JUDGE RANDALL'S
CHILDHOOD FRIEND

JUDGE RANDALL'S CHILDHOOD FRIEND

TONY ROGERS

A Judge Randall Mystery

Other titles in the Judge Randall series:

ISBN: 979-8-9864655-2-4 (Paperback)
ISBN: 979-8-9864655-3-1 (Ebook)

Published by Quinn Cove Books

Thanks to Joan Seymour for her invaluable editorial help.

Cover Design by Berge Design

To Tamara

1

Judge Randall sat on the edge of the bed, gradually coming to life. It always took longer than expected to decide if it were worth getting up. The natural gravitas of his face made him look depressed in the morning, when in actuality he was deep in thought, not depressed. Oh, sometimes he was, depressed, that is – Pat said he was and he trusted her – but most of the time he was simply trying to fit the pieces of the puzzle that is life into a meaningful whole before he got up.

The day was a milestone for him: he had been retired from the Massachusetts Superior Court for five years as of today. First thing he did was call Pat. Pat Knowles. They had served together as judges on the Superior Court and spent most nights together now that they were a couple.

"Good morning. Did you sleep well?"

"Yes. How about you?"

Jim walked to the bathroom holding the phone. "No, I tossed and turned."

"What was on your mind?" Pat's voice commanded attention, not because it was loud or harsh but because of its clarity and confidence.

"As of today I've been retired five years," Jim replied.

"What are your plans for the day?" Pat asked.

"A childhood friend of mine – George Holland – is joining me at The Long Gone. We lived two houses away from each other as kids and hung out together whenever we weren't in school. We were inseparable. His voice on the phone sounded like a road under repair; rough, after the gravel has been spread but before asphalt has been poured. Hard to connect the voice with the George I remember."

"What was he like as a boy?"

"Got along with everybody, neither a leader or a follower. Good natured, not a hostile bone in his body. You know how some boys enjoy pulling wings off flies? George would cry if another boy did. He owns a successful contracting company in Somerville and has for many years. It'll be good to see him."

"Does he have an agenda?"

"To see an old friend."

"But why now after all these years?"

Jim shrugged. "Do old friends need an excuse to get together?"

*

Jim didn't immediately recognize the heavyset man who walked into The Long Gone early the next morning. At that hour, Jim's favorite coffee shop did mostly takeout business but the all day lap toppers were starting to settle in; coffee houses were shared office spaces long before co-working became trendy.

The heavyset man hesitated at the door, as if looking for someone. When he spotted Jim, he stepped forward. He looked imposing but not intimidating.

"Are you Jim Randall?" The question seemed reluctant, as if he was afraid of the answer.

"I am."

The man stuck out his hand. "George Holland."

Jim got to his feet. "I wouldn't have recognized you, George."

"I recognized you. You look the same. Well, almost the same." George slapped Jim's shoulder.

"Nonsense, I look ancient. I am ancient, I turn seventy next month. Sit down. But first order at the counter."

George swiveled his head. "Where?"

"Where the sign says 'Order Here.'"

"Be right back."

Jim watched George go. Jim hadn't seen him since George's family moved away when George was ten and Jim was nine. Their childhood friendship had been effortless, natural, flowing from house to house, backyard to backyard. George's backyard included a basketball net and they spent hours shooting baskets. Jim never had a friendship like it again. Twenty-one years on the bench had reinforced his tendency to be a loner and Jim's friendships now came with borders and fences.

George returned to the table cradling what looked like a cup of steam but presumably contained liquid of some sort. "How are you, Jim?" he asked, sitting across from Jim.

"Grumpy but alive."

"Married?"

"Was. Joyce passed away six years ago. How about you, George?"

"Married twice. First wife died suddenly at the age of thirty-five, my brief second marriage to an unstable young woman named Pamela ended in divorce when she became pregnant by another man. Pamela was nineteen when we married, I was forty. An impulsive marriage, wrong from day one, but she was a knockout and I was lonely. Pamela's child, Sissy, is now an adult living in Wellesley. She's the polar opposite of her mother. No flash, no flair. If Pamela defines artifice, Sissy defines authentic. She's not my child so I rarely see her, but I like her when I do. It's really great to see you, Jim. I never had another friendship like ours."

"Same here."

Holland had the kind of wide body that make some people look jolly but made George look like a man who wanted to lie down. Jim tried to remember the young, affable George but couldn't, not with this George in front of him.

George's jocular voice defied the defeat in his body. "How the hell have you been, Jim? You've aged."

"Twenty-one years a judge will do that to you. I read somewhere that you own a contracting business."

"Yes, Holland Construction. Started it in my thirties but I'm tired, bone tired. I may sell the business to my office manager, Clyde Martin. Let him have the headaches. I'm over the hill. Do you understand what I'm saying?"

Jim grimaced. "I do. The only reason I'm not over the hill is because I can't get up the hill."

George smiled. When he smiled, he was the kid Jim remembered.

"It's good to see you, George. How did you find me after all these years?"

"Sissy read a profile of you in the *Boston Globe* that said you backed the parole of a man you sent to prison for life. I admire that. The article mentioned that The Long Gone had become your de facto office. Sissy said the story made you sound quirky and charming. She asked if you were the childhood friend I've talked about."

"I object. I have never been quirky or charming in my life. Opinionated, obstinate, and ornery, yes. Quirky and charming? I shudder. Why did you seek me out today, George? Not that it's not a pleasure."

George looked around the coffee shop as if to get his bearings. The Long Gone had little to no embellishment. Wooden tables and chairs, a chest-high ordering counter, a rest room near the rear: a place for study, contemplation, and good coffee. George took Jim's question as a challenge and grew defensive. "Do you object? Is it wrong to want to see my childhood friend again?"

"Of course not, George. Relax, I'm delighted to see you. I just wonder what you have on your mind. Twenty-one years as a judge will do that."

George's face darkened. "Sorry, I'm touchy as hell these days. Long story short: my ex-wife Pamela is being released from prison tomorrow and she is one scary woman."

Jim frowned. "Scary how?"

"Pamela's been in prison for assaulting her latest boyfriend. Fractured an eye socket. She had been in and out of trouble as a juvenile. Vandalism, truancy, that sort of thing. She is full-blown nuts, Jim. Goes from coquettish to cut-throat in one second flat. Can I stay with you until the danger passes?"

"Stay with me?"

"Yes. Hide out at your place. She knows where I live, but she doesn't know where you live."

"Why do you think she's after you?"

"Her angry letters from prison: 'It's all your fault. Everything's been downhill since you divorced me. All men want me, few reject me. Those who do pay the price.'"

Jim hesitated. Something about George's request struck Jim as strange, a little off, but George's fear was genuine, of that Jim had no doubt. "Sure, George. In honor of our childhood friendship, you're welcome to stay with me until you feel safe."

George brightened. "Thanks, Jim! I knew I could count on you."

George moved in right away. His luggage filled both the trunk and backseat of his car.

"George, I have to be honest. I hope you're not planning to settle in for the long haul."

George clapped Jim on the back. "Don't worry, old friend. I'll move out as soon as Pamela cools down."

Tall and narrow, Jim's Cambridge townhouse had a basement bedroom where guests could stay without being seen or heard. Jim so rarely had guests that the basement was pristine.

"This is great," George exclaimed when Jim showed him where he would stay. "I'm very grateful. No kidding."

Jim smiled wanly. "My pleasure. My companion Pat Knowles stays with me most nights or I stay at her Beacon Hill apartment. I don't know how you'll take to her. She's no nonsense but as true as anyone could be."

George was still surveying the room where he would sleep. "I'm sure I'll like her," he said off-handedly.

*

Pamela was released from prison on schedule. It took her less than a week to find Jim and George.

The doorbell rang at dinnertime. Jim and George were eating takeout from the local market when the doorbell rang.

Pamela stood in the doorway, looking ready to charm or kill. "You must be Judge Randall. I'm Pamela Holland. Is my delightful, disappointing, and thoroughly exasperating ex-husband hiding out at your place?"

Jim heard George's voice behind him.

"Hello, Pamela. Here I am."

Pamela shoved Jim aside. "May I come in? Hello, George, my darling ex-husband whom I wasn't good enough for. You look awful."

"And you look as ravishing as always, Pamela. How old are you now? Forty? Forty-five? Prison didn't dull your luster one bit."

Pamela beamed. "Still with the bullshit, George. You haven't changed."

Jim intervened. "Let's sit down in the living room, shall we? How did you find me?"

"Sissy found out where you live. I'm staying at her house until I find a place to stay. How could she refuse? Her grandparents may have raised her, but I am her birth mother." Pamela sat in Jim's favorite chair. "So you are the renowned Judge Randall. You've got fans on the inside. Tough but fair is the consensus of the incarcerated."

George turned to Jim. "Hear that, Jim? You've got a fan club."

Jim sat on the sofa. "A captive fan club. Doesn't count."

Pamela laughed loudly. Her laugh approached a bray. "Good for you, Judge! I like a man who can make fun of himself." She curled her legs beneath her.

George seemed cowed around her. "What are your plans, Pamela?"

"Plans?" She grinned. "Plans are for dweebs and losers." She broke into song. "Plans, I have a few, but then again too few to mention! Are you married, Judge?"

"Was. For a long time."

"Widowed or divorced?"

"The former."

Pamela seemed genuinely contrite. "I'm sorry. I hear losing a spouse is rough. George couldn't handle me. I don't blame him, few men could. We divorced after...how long was it, George? Six months? I blamed you at first, but I eventually forgave you. No one can say I lack compassion." Big smile. "Oh, look at the time! Sissy is expecting me. Can't you at least say it's been good to see me?" Pamela gave George a wry smile.

"It's been good to see you, Pamela."

Pamela stood and kissed George on the cheek. "You must work on your acting skills, George." She nodded at Jim. "A pleasure to meet you, Judge Randall. Goodbye for now."

The decompression in the room after she left was startling.

*

During the first week George stayed with Jim, George invited Jim to visit his office to see the company he had built.

"I want you to meet my office manager, Clyde Martin, and my personal assistant, Miriam Summers. They keep the office running."

Holland Construction, Somerville, MA, was housed in three trailers in a maze of streets on the corner of hidden and hard-to-find. The only identification of what the trailers housed was a small sign on the front door of the first.

"Hello, Miriam," George called when he and Jim walked in the door.

A gray-haired woman with a gentle face and an in-charge manner jumped to her feet at the front desk. Jim guessed her to be in her early sixties, but she could be younger or older; hard to tell. "George! Where have you been?"

"Hiding until the coast was clear. Jim, this is Miriam Summers, the indispensable Miriam. Miriam, this is my dear friend Jim Randall, former judge of the Massachusetts Superior Court. We go back to childhood."

Miriam shook Jim's hand with firm handshake and steady gaze. "You've known George all these years? Lucky you."

Jim couldn't read her tone: was she being sarcastic or adoring? "George and I lost touch after childhood. It's great to connect again."

Miriam addressed George. "Are you back to stay, George?"

"Unless you want to buy the business, Miriam." George winked at Jim.

Miriam blushed. "You have piles of work on your desk, George. Get to work, and don't disappear like that again. Clyde's been holding the fort, but we missed you."

As if on cue, a fifty-something man with a baby face and slumped shoulders walked into the reception area, greeted George properly but not warmly and shook Jim's hand. "You must be Judge Randall. I've heard about you."

"And you must be Clyde Martin."

"I am. George, your office is ready and waiting for you. Glad you're back."

"I'm not here for long today, but I'll be back to stay in a few days."

Clyde nodded. "Good. I've done the best I can while you've been gone, but I'm not you."

"Be thankful for small favors," George laughed. "I'll just show Jim my office, then we'll be on our way." George turned to Jim. "Okay?"

"Whatever you say."

George's office was cluttered with blueprints and hard-hats. A working office, not a showroom. "My inner sanctum."

"Impressive."

George chuckled. "What do you think of Clyde and Miriam?"

"Miriam is in love with you. Clyde patronizes you."

"I don't feel love from Miriam, I feel impatience. And Clyde is sure he can do a better job than me – which is probably true – but he sucks it up for the sake of our business. He has an MBA, unlike self-made me. Whatever Clyde's feelings towards me, he does an excellent job of running the day-to-day business. I could stay away forever and our customers and suppliers wouldn't notice – he's that good."

"Every small business needs a Clyde and a Miriam," Jim said.

George took a long last look around his office. "It's good to be back. Seen enough?" he asked Jim.

They bid goodbye to Miriam on their way out. Clyde was nowhere to be seen. "See you soon, Miriam," George called.

"We were worried about you, George. Don't disappear again."

The jocular George reappeared and jauntily waved goodbye. "Don't worry! You can't get rid of me that easily!"

Jim and George walked out of the office into the maze of streets. "Great gal," George said. "Old school. Hard to find someone like her nowadays."

"Both Miriam and Clyde seemed surprised to see you. Did they not know when you were coming back?"

"I told them I needed time to clear my head. I didn't give them a return date. They respected that."

They walked across the Cambridge/Somerville line to Jim's townhouse near Harvard Square. While Jim unlocked his door, George said, "I really appreciate your letting me stay with you, Jim. You didn't have to. I promise I won't stay any longer than necessary."

They stepped inside the house. "Good to meet Clyde and Miriam. You're lucky to have them."

"I couldn't agree more. They're irreplaceable."

2

Jim was still in bed when George called two mornings later. His friend's voice betrayed nothing out of the ordinary.

"Jim, it's George. I'm at the office. I came in early to get started on my backlog of work and found Clyde Martin dead in his office. I called 911. What else should I do?"

"Back up. Clyde Martin is dead?"

"Yes. Stabbed to death, a pool of blood on the floor. Wait, I hear sirens. It must be the police. I'll call you later, Jim."

Jim was technically awake but his awareness wasn't. Had a friend he had not seen since childhood, a friend who had slept in his basement for the past week, just calmly reported that his business manager had been stabbed to death? A bad dream most likely. Couldn't be real.

Jim got out of bed and went downstairs to the kitchen. What time was it? The wall clock said 6:30. Too early to call Ted Conover, his longtime adversary/friend in the DA's office. Or Pat, who had spent the night at her Beacon Hill apartment.

He made himself coffee and checked his overnight email. Nothing out of the ordinary. Holy hell broke loose at 8. Call after call. George again, then Pat. Then Sasha, Jim's reporter friend from the *Boston Globe*. Then George again. "The police are still here, Jim. This is awful. Just awful. My company won't survive this."

"Don't think about that now, George. Have the police estimated a time of death yet?"

"Sometime in late afternoon."

"He was still alive when you and I left the office, so presumably he was killed after that."

"*Yes*. That's obvious for Christ's sake!"

"My brain wakes up slowly, George."

"Sorry. I'm not myself."

"Who can blame you. Does Miriam know?"

"I called her at home and told her the police were here. She's coming in now. The police want to question her."

Jim took himself to The Long Gone earlier than usual. He didn't like The Long Gone before the morning rush. One could see how bare-bones the room was, how basic the tables and chairs. He ordered a dark roast at the counter and took it to a table close to the front windows. The street was lively at that hour even if The Long Gone wasn't. When George called a second time, the morning's settle-in crowd filled most of the coffee shop except the rear tables near the rest room. Laptops were out in full force.

George sounded exceptionally rattled. "They suspect me, Jim! The police think *I* killed Clyde!"

"Did you?"

"*No*, Jim. I swear to you, I didn't."

"Did you tell that to the police?"

"Yes, but they don't believe me. They don't outright say so, but I can tell. Will you vouch for me?"

"Of course, George."

"I didn't do it, Jim. I *swear* to you."

"I'm just thinking out loud. Do you have a lawyer?"

"Holland Construction has one to handle our business matters, but she's not a criminal attorney. Can you help me, Jim?"

Jim shook his head a firm 'no', which George couldn't see. "I'm not going to be your lawyer, George. If you are suspected, you'll need an experienced criminal lawyer. Are the police still there?"

"Yes."

"I'll come and vouch for you personally. That's as much as I feel comfortable doing."

"*Thank you*, Jim." George sounded relieved.

Jim drove to the short distance to George's office. The police detective on the scene had deep lines on his forehead that announced to all he met: 'You're lying.' He introduced himself: "Detective Jenkins. I'm speaking to a legal legend," he said without looking Jim in the eye.

"A relic, not a legend," Jim corrected.

"Clyde Martin was stabbed twice. Once in the shoulder, once in the heart. We think he and his assailant knew each other. What's your interest in the case?"

"George Holland and I were best friends as kids. He reached out to me recently wanting to renew our friendship. He called early this morning to tell me of Clyde Martin's death."

"We've taken your friend to headquarters for questioning. What was his demeanor over the phone?"

"Borderline frantic. Holding it together out of a sense of duty. I didn't recognize his voice at first."

"To your knowledge, had your friend ever threatened Clyde Martin?"

"Not to my knowledge, no. The George I knew was a sweet guy. He cried when anyone he knew got hurt. Do you suspect him for the murder?"

"You know the drill, Judge. Everyone's a suspect until ruled out."

"And everyone's innocent until proven guilty."

"Yes, Judge. We know. We'll take it from here. All due respect."

Jim didn't linger. He walked towards home remembering only after he left the maze of streets that he had driven to George's office. When he retraced his steps to retrieve his car, all but one of the police cars had gone.

Jim's living room, which seemed ordinary to him most of the time, seemed obscenely comfortable under the circumstances. He sat in his favorite chair visualizing Clyde Martin being stabbed to death in his office.

He reached for his phone.

"Pat, it's me."

"What's wrong? You sound awful."

"Clyde Martin has been murdered. You heard me correctly. I just returned home after telling the police what I know, which is very little. I'm back in my living room, trying to accept that I didn't imagine this morning, wishing I had."

Jim was still immobile in his chair an hour later. When at last he stirred, he called Ted Conover, longtime Assistant District Attorney, frequent presence in Jim's courtroom and good friend since Jim's retirement. "Ted, it's Jim Randall."

"Are you calling about Clyde Martin's murder?"

"Word travels fast. How did you hear?"

"Sasha Cohen of the *Globe* called soon after the police report came in. George Holland is, or was, Clyde Martin's boss, correct? And you and George Holland are friends, or were, is that right?"

"Inseparable as kids. I hadn't talked to him in decades until a few days ago. I spent this morning at his office telling the detective investigating the murder what I know. Jenkins, I think it was. Detective Jenkins. I don't think Detective Jenkins believes me."

"Apparently Jenkins got under your skin. That's not like you, Jim my friend."

"For obvious reasons I don't have my usual distance on this case. Do you know Jenkins?"

"Only by reputation. Old school is what I hear."

"I distrust people whose default position is distrust. He partially ditched the attitude by the time I left him, I have to acknowledge."

"He gets results. Back to the murder, Jim. What do you know about it?"

"Nothing other than what George told me. That he found Clyde Martin dead in the office this morning."

"Nothing else?"

"He was too rattled to say much more."

Jim went to his kitchen, not to get coffee or something to eat, but to fully wake up. He wanted to call Sasha Cohen at the *Globe* but wanted a clear head when he talked to her.

He got her voice mail. "Sasha, it's Jim Randall. Call me."

Sasha had been an eager young reporter for a local weekly when Jim met her. He had championed her move to the *Globe*. She called back quickly and didn't give Jim a chance to talk before she did. "A man named Clyde Martin who worked for Holland Construction was stabbed to death in his office last night. Is that why you called me?"

"Yes, that's why I called. George Holland and I were childhood friends. He recently reached out to me after many years. First question: how did you hear?"

"It's my job to hear. What do you know so far?"

"That George Holland is innocent."

"And you know that how?"

"We were fast friends as kids. He literally wouldn't hurt a fly. Let's meet at The Long Gone. This topic requires more than a phone call."

"I'm a little busy, Jim."

"You'll want to talk to me, Sasha. Consider me a source, someone who met Clyde Martin and grew up with George Holland."

"I'm hooked. Later this morning?"

"Fine with me. We might have to sit by the rest room at that hour but so be it."

Sasha got to The Long Gone at 11. Jim had been right, the only empty table was in the short corridor leading to the unisex restroom and the emergency exit. Jim had lingered at the table many times when he wanted to be alone and always took some amusement from seeing the faces of the patrons emerging from the rest room and realizing that Jim had clearly heard their flush and farts. 'It's okay,' he wanted to tell them, 'I'm on the job.'

Sasha sat down without seeming to notice the location. She had the quick movements of someone with a mental checklist and no time to waste. "Talk fast, Jim. I've got sources to meet and stories to write."

"Who are you meeting?"

"An MIT Nobel Laureate in physics who doesn't like to be kept waiting."

"Back on earth I can tell you that George Holland is the last person I would suspect for breaking the law. Hard even to imagine him parking in a no-parking zone."

"Which means he's probably the killer."

"Don't be jaded, Sasha."

"I'm only following the journalist's rule book."

A harried-looking woman ducked into the restroom. Sasha continued without noticing. "What I want to know is whether you picked up vibes of office troubles, squabbles, fights, tensions, when you visited."

"No, but keep in mind I only visited the office once."

"You met Clyde Martin?"

"Just to say hello."

"You have good instincts, Jim. Give me your impression of him."

"Competent at his job, pissed at George for holding him back."

"How about Miriam Summers, the receptionist. What was your impression of her?"

"That she fiercely guards the gates, nothing gets by her. She and Clyde make a formidable team."

"Past tense, Jim. Past tense."

"I stand corrected. Made a formidable team. She and Clyde made a formidable team."

"That's better. And finally, Pamela Holland, George Holland's ex-wife. What's your impression of her?"

"Now there's a person who has so thoroughly molded herself to please the men in her life that little is left of the real Pamela. My sense is that what's left is emerging now that she has served her time. And all I can say is, world watch out."

Sasha leaned back to study Jim. "In the relatively short time I've known you, you have evolved from judge to psychologist. Did you know that?"

Jim said, "A good judge is by definition part-psychologist."

Sasha paused. "Where were we?"

"Your story for the *Globe*. What's your angle going to be?"

"Don't know yet. Pamela Holland is the wild card – just out of prison, used to manipulating men, vengeful when her manipulations fail. Maybe she came to the office to take revenge against George and killed Clyde when he interfered."

"Doesn't ring true. If she intended to kill George, George would be dead by now."

"I want to know more about Clyde Martin. Why would anyone want to stab to death a man who was good at his job, who kept his head down, who made no discernable waves?"

The toilet flushed. Metaphor? The woman emerged, clawing through her handbag. She bumped into Jim's elbow. "Excuse me. Sorry. Can't find my keys," muttered as she hurried away.

Jim chuckled. "That's fate telling us to cut the crap.."

They didn't linger at The Long Gone much longer. Sasha went to her office and Jim ate lunch at the diner across the street. Inman Square was evolving but had as yet avoided going full-Harvard Square. Jim was to meet Pamela Holland at The Long Gone later but had time to kill. He killed it by walking to Beauty Shop Row, his favorite part of Cambridge Street. The variety of languages and storefronts, of life lived at street level, never failed to please. Although maybe someday someone would explain to him how eyebrows could be threaded.

When Pamela burst into the coffee shop later that afternoon, she looked so out-of-place – heavy eyeshadow, purple-red lips – that patrons who happened to glance up from their laptops were startled. In Cambridge one doesn't call attention to one's looks if one wants to be taken seriously. She spotted Jim quickly and sat down across from him. "I feel uncomfortable, everyone's staring at me."

"You like attention, don't you?"

"Not when people look at me as if I'm some kind of freak. Why on earth do you like this place?"

"It's democratic, with a small d. Everyone is welcome."

"Oh, good. They've stopped staring. I can be myself." She sat back in her chair, still looking out-of-place.

"I asked you here to talk about Clyde Martin. I think you know the sad news?"

Pamela's face fell; for real this time, not for show. "George told me. Hard to imagine anyone wanting to kill Clyde."

"How well did you know him?"

"No one knew him well. That's the kind of man he was. But I liked and respected him, which is rare for me. He was working for George when George and I were married. Always got his job done. Never made waves." She faltered. "Did you see his body? Was it awful?"

"I didn't. I was told the scene was bloody."

That brought Pamela to tears. "Why would anyone want to hurt Clyde? I have a heart, in spite of what others think, and I can't imagine anyone hating Clyde enough to kill him."

"Your tears tell me he meant a lot to you."

Pamela shook her head. "My, my. I had heard so much about you − the legendary Judge Randall − that I thought you'd be different. But you're not. Not at all."

"Explain what you mean by that. I'm a little slow in old age."

"No, you're not, but men are men. Sex is never out of your minds for long. To be explicit and despite your suspicions, I never fucked Clyde. George and I were married when I knew Clyde; I am outrageous but not unfaithful."

"How many times have you been in prison?"

"Just this once, but I did time in juvie for shoplifting and truancy."

"George was your first husband, correct?"

"Yes. His first wife had died and he was alone in a way he never had been before. An amiable guy like George doesn't know how to cope with that kind of loneliness. Then along came lil' ol' me. He had never been with a woman like me. I think I overwhelmed his defenses. By the way, to give you the full picture, I don't actually like sex all that much, I just wield it."

"Interesting that you know that about yourself, you don't give the impression of being an introspective woman. Any chance you and George will get back together now that you've paid your dues to society?"

What happened next stunned Jim. Pamela stood so abruptly that she knocked down her chair. It clattered as it fell, drawing attention. She noticed the attention, but apparently it wasn't the kind she liked because she bolted from The Long Gone with a metaphorical huff and puff. When she was gone, the attention turned to Jim. What had such a colorful woman been doing with such a colorless man, and what had he said to drive her away? Jim felt self-conscious. He liked to be the observer, not the observed. In his judicial robe on his judge's bench, he had never felt self-conscious but this morning, in his hangout, his de facto office, he did. He quickly left The Long Gone, trying his best to recreate sweeping out of his courtroom.

What had set Pamela off? He asked Pat's opinion that evening in her apartment. The red brick of Beacon Hill was vivid through her windows. "Pamela and I were having a civilized if not chummy conversation, when she jumped to her feet and stormed out. What's your guess as to why?"

"Maybe she realized you had stopped buying her act?"

"No, she doesn't hide the fact that her facade is a useful tool, a way to get what she wants. I don't think she was offended that I see through it. I think she is amazed most men don't, she's not an ingénue."

Pat tried again. "Maybe the hint of her repeat marriages is what set her off."

"That could be."

"Jim, as smart as you are, as good a judge of character, I don't think you are equipped to deal with a woman like Pamela."

He spread his hands. "Guilty as charged, but I did okay this time, I think."

"Don't get defensive. Every man in the world is distracted by surfaces when it comes to women. We women know that. Sure, substance matters for some men some of the time, but as a rule, surfaces rule."

Jim mildly bristled. "Why do women have anything to do with us if we're so shallow?"

"Women are silly, men are simple. I rest my case."

3

Detective Jenkins did not seem happy to see Jim again. Police headquarters lacked bars but otherwise felt like prison. Maybe it was the patina of despair, of guilt. Jenkins emerged from the back offices when he was told Jim was looking for him.

"What can I do for you?" Jenkins asked without emotion, let alone interest in the answer.

"I've learned more about Clyde Martin's murder, specifically about Pamela Holland."

"Thanks, but I don't need amateur help."

Jim bristled. "I admit to being an amateur sleuth but I have twenty-one years of experience assessing the guilt or innocence of people who appeared before me in court, and I don't like being brushed off. You aren't even close to solving this case on your own, am I right?"

The invisible shield that detectives don to hide their vulnerability lowered just a bit, enough to reveal that Jenkins was human, attitude to the contrary. "Okay. What have you got?"

"Sorry to bristle but I get tired of attitudes. You often can tell what a person fears by their attitude, and you fear not being taken seriously, correct? I had a candid discussion with Pamela Holland. She's become comfortable enough with me to lower her guard just a bit. Want my opinion?"

"Yes, I do." Jenkins' tone said otherwise.

"Sound like you mean it."

"I want your opinion. *Please* give me your opinion."

That elicited a chuckle. "That's more like it. Pamela's not our killer. She's a lost little girl who's become trapped behind her facade."

Detective Jenkins raised an eyebrow. "What leads you to that opinion?"

"Pamela is an experienced actor. She only knows one role but she's very good at it. If she wanted to make a case that there was no one in the world less likely to murder than she, she would have no trouble doing so. Murder wasn't on her mind when she and I talked. Her waning powers as a femme fatale were more on her mind than murder."

"Let me get this straight. Because she didn't offer an alibi, she didn't do it? Is that what you're saying?"

"Because she didn't seem worried she'd be charged. She's a woman who has no trouble hiding whatever she wants to hide, so when she doesn't even try, I think she has nothing to hide."

Jim's reasoning made Jenkins grin, or was it a grimace? "Your reasoning is sui generis, to say the least."

Jim held up a hand. "I admit I could be wrong, not only wrong, but egregiously wrong. In your role you have to build a case on a foundation of fact, I can start with speculation, try ideas on for size, throw them out as necessary. Maybe we can help each other."

"Doubtful but intriguing enough that I'd like to explore your way of thinking over a beer sometime. In the meantime, your offer of help is noted." With a quick wave – of goodbye? of dismissal? – Jenkins disappeared into the back offices.

Jim's legs had stiffened while they talked, and he walked out of police headquarters as if on stilts. That had gone differently than expected. Had he screwed up? He hadn't planned to bristle, nor – Jim would bet – had Jenkins. Why are detectives, pro and am, touchier than suspects? And what is the meaning of life?

It was almost lunchtime. He was not far from Beacon Hill. He called Pat. "Lunch?" he asked when she answered her phone.

"Where do you have in mind? I'm not in the mood to come to Cambridge."

"I just left police headquarters. I could meet you in Back Bay or on Charles Street, if you like."

"Do I want to walk downhill to see you? That is the question."

"Okay, I'm smiling."

"There's a new place on Newbury Street, if you can force yourself to try someplace new."

"I'm always up for a change. Change is my middle name."

Pat couldn't stop laughing. "Jim Change Randall? Wait, I know. Change can be your rapper name. Rapper Jimmy Change!"

"Now I'm a rapper? In your dreams."

"Precisely." She was still laughing.

"Glad to cheer you up. What time shall we meet for lunch?"

"In forty-five minutes. That'll give me time to apply my makeup."

"You don't wear makeup."

"You're hung up on fact, aren't you?"

"When it comes to women and their makeup I insist on nothing less. Exhibit A: Pamela Holland."

"I am rethinking lunch."

"What's the name of this alleged place where you want to meet?"

Deadpan. "Nellie's Nothing Fancy."

"Really?"

"No, not really. Simone's Gourmet Pizza is the name." Her laugh was like the sputtering of an outboard motor as it slows to a stop.

"I distrust any place that calls itself 'gourmet'. I shall be the judge of that, I say."

"But?"

"For you, dear, anything."

"I am silently banging my gavel."

Jim rendered his verdict as they walked home after lunch. "Worst pizza I've ever had." During lunch he had given Pat a recap of his meeting with Detective Jenkins. Now he added an afterthought. "I thought I handled Jenkins well. What's wrong? Why do you have that expression on your face?"

"Be careful, Jim. You are having way too much fun."

"Why do I like thee?"

"And don't pout. You're a good judge of character. But you are acting like a kid let out of school. You're prone to make mistakes when you get carried away."

"I don't think I'm in danger of that."

"A poor choice of words on my part. But I don't believe you realize how – oh, I don't know – giddy you've seemed since George Holland reentered your life."

His laugh was on a three second time-delay. "Giddy? I seemed giddy? Hearing that makes me feel – oh, I don't know – giddy."

"Maybe I like it when you are giddy. Maybe it turns me on."

"You mean, it makes you horny?"

"You're words, not mine."

"I know, we can start a law firm, Giddy and Horny."

She groaned. "What kind of law does Giddy and Horny practice?"

"Estate planning? Taxation?"

"Walk faster. You walk like an old man."

"I do not. Property law? Labor law?"

"Stop jabbering and walk."

"Divorce law? Yes, that's it. Divorce law!"

"You're out of luck. We're not married."

"Facts, facts, and only the facts, eh, Judge Knowles?"

"Always, Rapper Jimmy."

*

Jim sat at the desk in his third-floor study staring out the window. The trees he saw looked different every time. Different but the same, a philosophical conundrum. What was the conundrum trying to tell him? Usually when Jim got absorbed in a case he couldn't think about anything else, let alone philosophical conundrums. He told himself he had lost his concentration because his childhood friend was involved. And because – he told himself – Detective Jenkins seemed competent; not friendly but good at his job. Ergo, Jim could take a back seat on this one.

And face it, his sell-by date as an amateur sleuth may have come and gone. He couldn't expect to go on solving crime forever.

Heed Pat's words. If she said he was in danger of getting carried away, he was. He wouldn't go as far as to call himself giddy, but she hadn't been serious. Had she?

Maybe he should 'retire' which being self-appointed made it easy to do. If he wanted to quit, that is. All he had to do was cease and desist. No bench to step down from, no robe to doff, no gavel to drop. Just stop. Turning seventy might be the time to do it.

Pat was in the kitchen. He went downstairs and found her preparing lunch.

"I'm thinking of retiring."

"From what?"

"Sleuthing."

"If that's what you want. I predict you'll be bored if you do."

"So you don't think I should?"

"I think it's up to you. Just consider all the consequences, pro and con."

Jim was too inhibited a man to throw up his hands, but in his imagination he threw them sky-high. "You're no help. I'm serious here."

"I know you are. And I'm saying I'll support whatever decision you make."

Jim went to the kitchen counter where there was an open bottle of red wine. He poured himself a glass. "Big help you are."

The wine was stale. He poured it into the sink.

"Let's take George to dinner at Duck, Duck, Goose."

"Fine with me."

"I think he'll like it."

"Let's do it."

"I'll invite him."

"Good."

"And to make it interesting, I'll invite Pamela to join us."

"Will George agree to that?"

"I think so. For a variety of reasons, not least of which is curiosity to see what's she's like now. I think he'll feel safe: you and I will be there, and we'll be in a restaurant surrounded by other people."

"Will Pamela agree to it?"

"Oh, yeah. Of that I have no doubt."

As they were getting ready for bed later that evening, Pat offered this suggestion. Make it harder for George to turn down the invitation by calling the dinner Jim's seventieth birthday celebration.

*

Bruce at Duck, Duck, Goose had Jim's favorite window table set for four when the party arrived. Pamela had agreed as soon as she was asked, George took a little time to say yes.

But he came. Wearing a coat and tie. Which Jim wasn't.

"Hello, Pamela," George said. His voice was neither annoyed nor glad.

"Hello, George."

They sat. Pat broke the ice. "I know this is awkward, but let's enjoy ourselves."

George brightened. "In honor of the new senior citizen amongst us."

"And for old friendships and past marriages."

Pamela added. "Thank you for inviting me. I know I'm the oddball, but I feel very comfortable here."

George reassured her. "A lot of water over the dam since our divorce, Pamela."

"Yes, George."

Pat had preordered a bottle of champagne for the table. Glasses were filled and raised.

"I propose a toast," George said. "To my childhood friend, Jim Randall, a really super guy. Your stern demeanor doesn't fool anybody, Jim. A toast then to Jim Randall. Too old for his own good but we still love him. Happy birthday, Jim." Glasses were clicked.

Jim replied. "Friendships don't always endure, so I'm especially delighted that George got back in touch with me after all these years. We've both aged, but I've aged better than him." Gentle laughter around the table. "Now let's enjoy ourselves. No talk of anything unpleasant. Gavel or no gavel, I will strictly enforce that rule."

The evening went smoothly. Pamela seemed to enjoy herself. Surprisingly she and Pat hit it off. On the walk home Jim was curious. "You two seemed to have a high ol' time. What did you talk about?"

"She's really not so bad once you get to know her."

"I never said she was."

"The world makes assumptions based on her appearance."

"You mean men, men make assumptions."

"Your words, not mine."

"Any hints about the murder?"

"None. I didn't expect any. Did you?"

"No, I didn't." They were almost at Jim's townhouse.

Pat summarized. "A good evening overall."

Jim got out his keys as they climbed the front steps. "Yes. A good evening."

4

Time for another visit to Holland Construction. Among Jim's investigating methods – to the extent he had methods – was to hang out at the scene of a crime and absorb whatever registered in his consciousness after he put aside his incessant to-do list. To be fully conscious without being self-conscious. Next to impossible in reality, but he was getting the hang of it. To be a good sleuth required a touch of zen.

Miriam was at the front desk. Her voice sounded robotic. Metallic. Bored. "Can I help you?"

"Judge Randall. Remember me?"

"Of course I remember you. You make an indelible impression. What do you want this time?" Her voice didn't soften.

"To hang out and observe a morning's comings and goings. No questions, no pressure. I'll become invisible."

Miriam stood from her desk. "Impossible."

"What's impossible? Hanging out in your office?"

She moved from behind her desk to stand in front of Jim. "No. Becoming invisible. You have a formidable presence, Judge. You are a physically imposing man."

"I shall do my best to be unimposing. Okay?"

Miriam surveyed her domain; a utilitarian reception room, a desk, four folding chairs, nothing on the walls. "Where would you like to hang out?"

"There." Jim pointed to a folding chair.

She nodded. "You won't be comfortable but be my guest. Shall I call George and tell him you're here? I expect him later this morning."

"No need. He won't be surprised I'm here."

Over the course of the next hour, Jim watched who came and went. There weren't many. A developer checking on a project, several tradespeople including an HVAC tech and a roofer, a woman looking for a pet store she had heard was nearby. George didn't appear until late morning.

He addressed Jim, "So you came. I wasn't sure you would. Learn anything?"

"I won't know until my impressions sort themselves at the end of the day, until I see what rises to the surface. Meanwhile Miriam has kept me out of trouble."

George smiled at her. "Nothing escapes Miriam. Now I've got work to do. You're welcome to join me in my office. It's more comfortable."

Jim stood. "I shall. Thank you. I won't stay long."

George's office was as cluttered as before. As George sat at his desk, he asked, "Have you talked to Pamela since our dinner together?"

"I've had no occasion to. Have you? Talked to her?"

"Yes."

"In a way, that surprises me. You two seemed barely on speaking terms."

"The dinner broke the ice. Made me remember why I married her. So I called her. Do you blame me? She's still attractive."

"I rarely blame anybody for who they like and dislike. We are all human."

George nodded. "Yes, so I called her. She and I are having dinner together in a few days. Can't be any harm in that, can there?"

"Yes, there can, but you know that. Be on alert."

"I shall." George fiddled with papers that were on his desk. "It's good to be in touch with you again, Jim. We can't fall out of touch in the future."

Jim smiled. "We won't let that happen, George."

"Jim, who killed Clyde?"

"No idea, but having felt for myself the cloistered atmosphere of Holland Construction, I think the killer works here, or had a relationship with someone who does."

"Like Pamela, you mean?"

"Goodbye, George."

Jim returned to the front office.

"Good to see you, Miriam. I'm sure we'll be seeing each other again."

"You're leaving? Did you get what you want?"

"I think so. I never know for sure until I reflect."

Miriam digested that. "I wish more people would think before they open their damn fool mouths. Clyde Martin was a good man, Judge, a very good man. No loose ends to that man. Straight talk or no talk. I admired him, do you hear? I *admired* him. Who would want to kill such an admirable man?" Miriam shuddered. Jim thought she might cry.

Jim said, "I've upset you. I'm sorry. I'll leave you alone."

"Judge, please find whoever murdered my Clyde. *Please!* Do you think it's someone at Holland Construction?"

"Yes, or someone who has or had a personal relationship with someone at the company."

"If that's true, I'll never feel safe here again."

Jim went to the door. "Thank you for allowing me to invade your space. I know you prefer to be alone."

Miriam wasn't done. "Clyde was one of the finest people I have ever known."

"Understood."

"I mean it." Miriam seemed lost in memories. "I feel like crying when I think I'll never be able to walk the few steps to his office and see him at his desk."

"I'll do my best to find whoever did it. I promise."

Jim walked out into the tiny streets of the small industry district, feeling clumsy. A bull in a china shop, that's what he was. Breaking china was sometimes a prerequisite to solving a case, but Miriam was a lonely woman entitled to her dreams.

*

Jim couldn't cook: a store-bought roast chicken, pre-washed salad, and an artisan loaf of bread was a gourmet meal for Jim. No potatoes. Jim would never be slim but he did not want to balloon up like so many old timers.

Pat cooked but didn't enjoy it. Cook, eat, clean. Done for the night.

Though Jim couldn't cook, he considered himself a consummate dishwasher (although Pat said he didn't scrub the pots thoroughly enough).

"I hung out at Holland Construction this morning," Jim said while Pat cleared and he scrubbed after a dinner Pat cooked.

Pat replied, "Discover anything?"

"A lonely woman and a guilty man."

"Are you talking about Miriam and George? You think George is guilty?"

"Not necessarily of Clyde Martin's murder, but of something. Whatever it is has turned him inside out. Same good guy on the surface, tortured underneath."

"Tortured?"

"That may be extreme. Troubled, guilt ridden."

Pat mulled that over for a minute. "From what I've heard, the construction business can be brutal. Maybe that's all it is. He's taken his eyes off the ball and feels guilty about it. By the way, I think Pamela will try to seduce you with the purpose of distracting you from her role in Clyde's murder."

"Not because of my irresistible charm, Judge Knowles?"

"Scrub harder, Judge Randall. You've missed a spot or two."

*

The afternoon contingent at The Long Gone skewed older: grad school students, mothers grabbing a moment to themselves before their kids got home from school, old folks with Einstein hair. Jim preferred the morning crowd: college kids trying to wake up, tradespeople buying coffee to take with them on the job, the stray professor reviewing her lecture notes before class.

Ernie Farrell was to meet Jim at The Long Gone. Ernie was the tech wizard Jim had represented in Jim's first post-judicial foray back into the courts. Ernie entered The Long Gone with as little fanfare as was humanly possible, the polar opposite of Pamela Holland's grand entrance.

"How goes it?" Ernie asked, sitting across from Jim.

"Not bad. Yourself?"

Ernie jumped back up. "I always forget to order my coffee before I sit."

Ernie returned with a tall takeout cup of coffee. "There," sitting back down. "Much better. How are you?"

"Fine, Ernie. How have you been?"

"Paranoid as always but otherwise fine. Is this a social visit? That's not like you."

"This is me trying to be nice before I get down to business."

Ernie smiled. He had one of those smiles that seem rusty but genuine; heartfelt but seldom used. "Judge, no one meets face-to-face anymore. Friendships take place in two-dimensions. You – being three-dimensional – are an anachronism. No offense."

"None taken, in fact I take pride in being three-dimensional. My third dimension is my best. 3-D glasses not needed."

"That's what I like about you."

"My modesty?"

"Your sense of humor. It's so well-hidden."

Jim feigned hurt feelings. "I consider myself a laugh riot."

"You asked me here today for a purpose. What is it?"

"I'd like your opinion. Let's say you run a business with lots of tradespeople and only a few staff, most of them long-term employees. Then let's say your right-hand man is found stabbed to death in his office. What would be your first step in finding the killer?"

"I'd ask an amateur-sleuth, ex-judge with a seldom-used sense of humor named Randall to investigate."

"And where would you expect this humorless sleuth to start?"

"How well does he know the employees?"

"He and the owner were boyhood friends."

"Then he's probably not the best person to take the case."

"I agree. But let's say he feels he owes his friend. Here are the facts: the outside security camera shows no one entering the offices after working hours. Odds are it was an inside job, but it could have been the ex-wife of the owner who had recently been released from prison after serving time for assault. The security camera showed her stopping by the offices just before five and leaving at ten after five. George Holland, the owner, left the office at five thirty, and the receptionist, Miriam Summers, hurriedly left at a quarter to six. What said sleuth observed when he spent time in the office was how everyone tiptoed around the receptionist: the clients who came to check on their projects, the tradespeople who checked in before going out on the job, the UPS guy who moved at warp speed but still had time for a nod and a quip. A front office run by a demanding aunt whom no one dare cross."

"Does the murdered man appear on the video?"

"The murdered man's name was Clyde Martin. He appears on the video arriving in the morning, but isn't seen leaving."

Ernie looked at Jim.

"Why the stare?" Jim asked.

"Your story omits the obvious conclusion."

"What conclusion?"

"The receptionist did it."

"Miriam had no need to kill. She gets her way by other means. Besides, she's not a young woman. She's an unlikely person to stab a man to death."

Ernie shrugged. "I'm just drawing the logical conclusion from the facts you presented."

"Logical but not persuasive, if you know Miriam. She takes great pride in being the ringmaster. Why would she kill one of the key members of her troupe?"

"Judge, relax, I'm just trying ideas on for size. That's what you asked me here to do, right? She was the last person to leave the office, and Clyde Martin was not seen leaving for the night for the very good reason that he had been murdered. Correct so far?"

"Yes, but what I can't wrap my head around is why a mother hen like Miriam would murder a dependable longtime employee like Clyde," Jim said.

"Unrequited love? She was in love with Clyde and he brushed her off? Imagine how that would sting."

"I'm not persuaded. Miriam is a person who keeps her emotions under lock and key. She wouldn't lash out with deadly force."

"Then who? You're the amateur detective, I'm the tech guru."

"Actually, I'm the rapper."

"Excuse me?" Ernie asked, puzzled.

"Never mind. Some puzzles are best left unsolved."

*

Jim recapped his day for Pat that evening. "I admit to being more troubled than usual by this case. I've let my personal feelings get involved."

Pat put her own spin on it. "When we were judges and could gavel the court to order, it gave us an illusion of control. Now that we don't have even an illusion of control, it's scary."

"Leaving that aside, Pat, what's your guess who killed Clyde?"

"I'd put my money on Pamela. She gets out of prison, Clyde dies. I sense that's not a coincidence."

"But the security camera doesn't support that. And what was her motive?"

"Were Pamela and Clyde ever an item? Was she hoping to rub George's face in what he threw away when he divorced her?"

"That's a leap too far for a seventy-year-old man to make. Maybe sleuthing is best left to the young," Jim said.

Jim was scheduled to pay a visit to Detective Jenkins in the morning and wanted to be mentally sharp, but he slept fitfully. Do the best you can, Jim, he told himself.

Police headquarters still depressed Jim. A place where dreams went to die. Detective Jenkins came out to greet him. The lines in his forehead looked deeper than ever. His smile was simultaneously sincere and a sneer ."I'm not a gossip columnist," he replied in answer to Jim's question. "How the hell should I know whether Clyde Martin and Pamela Holland were ever an item?"

"Bear with me, please. Any forensic evidence pointing to the killer?"

"No. All the people who left fingerprints in the Holland Construction office belong there. Employees or tradespeople. Most of the fingerprints belong to George and Miriam." Jenkins face switched from know-it-all to that's-all-I-got. "What's your take so far?"

Jim spread his hands. "I'm hedging my bets. Pat Knowles – ex-judge Pat Knowles, my significant other and alter ego – thinks Pamela Holland, George's flamboyant second wife, did it, but I'm not convinced."

Jenkins' face took on the look of a student caught smoking weed by a take-no-prisoners teacher. "I wish killers would make our jobs easier. I'll compile a list of clues to leave at crime scenes."

Jim smiled. "Criminals could be more helpful than they are."

"Wouldn't that be wonderful?" Jenkins gave a wistful smile before his face closed down again.

In Jim's experience, truly tough guys – Jenkins wasn't one – were rare but scary when encountered. One nineteen year old who had appeared before Jim in court had been caught by his eighty-four year old grandmother stealing from her purse, so the teenager broke her skull and left her for dead. He netted eight dollars and change. Jim remembered being scared to have him in his courtroom even though they were separated by the judge's bench and court officers. Truly mean guys were, in Jim's experience, rare. Detective Jenkins was hardened by his job but not nasty by nature, if Jim read him correctly.

Jim left police headquarters grateful for the legal system, as flawed as it was. When the guilty were caught and convicted, it was something of a miracle given how many things could go wrong (Jim realized he had lost track of where his feet were stepping – this is when old folks fall and break a hip, he warned himself). Suddenly Jim was grateful for everyone involved in the legal system: grateful for cops (most of them at least), grateful for judges (likewise), grateful for jurors, who for the most part take their duties as jurors very seriously. When you think about twelve strangers with no legal background being thrown together to collectively decide the fate of other total strangers, it is something of a miracle that things ever go right. Which they do a majority of the time, in his experience. It's fun to grumble about the legal system's shortcomings, but it's also important to acknowledge what works.

He let his legs do his thinking while he pulled out his phone to call Sissy.

Sissy answered. Jim imagined her sitting in her comfortable living room.

"Sissy, this is Jim Randall. Good morning."

"Good morning, Judge Randall. Are you looking for Pamela? She's out of the house but I expect her back shortly."

"She's still staying with you?"

"Yes, until she finds a place of her own. Do you want her to call you back?"

"No, she doesn't have to bother. I just want to know where she is, in case I need to be in touch. I have a feeling that will be soon."

"Very well." Sissy hesitated, unsure what to say next. "Has Clyde Martin's killer been caught?"

"Not yet."

"From what I knew of Clyde, all he wanted was to do his job and go home to his cats. A hard man to know but admired by all. Why would anyone want to kill him?"

"We may never know. As long as human beings are the ones committing the crimes, crime doesn't need a reason."

Jim made it home without falling. Going to the kitchen he poured himself a congratulatory glass of Côtes du Rhône, rare for midday. Leaning against his kitchen counter, sipping his wine, he felt exhausted. What was happening to him? The morning hadn't been hard, the walk to the Park Street T and from Harvard Square to his townhouse hadn't been long. He knew what Pat would say, age was happening to him. He thought rather that his fatigue was the result of worry about his friend George. Jim had a bad feeling about George. He would hate – absolutely hate – to have the memory of his childhood friendship tarnished. He would *especially* hate being the one who tarnished it. But he had a bad feeling.

Jim was sitting in his most comfortable chair when Sasha Cohen called. "Jim, I think this might interest you."

"What would?"

"Cone of silence, Jim. We're only getting bits and pieces of the story so the *Globe* isn't ready to go to press with it, but as a friend who cares about you and knows you are investigating Holland Construction, I wanted to give you a heads-up."

"I'm listening." He really, really, didn't want to stir.

"A balcony collapse in Woburn led our Spotlight Team to investigate. They uncovered a scheme involving several contractors using faulty materials in the construction of suburban homes leading to several instances of collapse or near-collapse. We're working with the DA's office to determine which contractors are involved. My gut tells me this will be big once the investigation wraps up."

"Is Holland Construction one of them? Is that why you're telling me?"

"Nothing definite mind you but early indications are that Holland Construction was an early adopter of the scheme. I'm telling you this as a friend and as someone who's helped me in the past, but you are not to tell anyone. Not even Pat. This is explosive and the *Globe* wants to get it right before we go public."

"My lips are sealed. Is George Holland personally implicated?"

"That I can't tell you."

"Can't or won't?"

"Both, Jim. Don't let me down, keep this to yourself. Don't even talk to the DA. I don't want him to know I've told you. If you leak this story, I'll never share information with you again."

"Sasha, I get it."

"Good. I'll alert you if and when we're ready to go public."

"What you've told me is scary. Deaths may already have resulted."

"Now you get why this is so explosive. I ask as you investigate Clyde Martin's murder, if you learn anything that's relevant to our investigation, I would appreciate your letting me know."

"So you think they are connected? Clyde Martin's murder and the scheme you've uncovered?"

"I don't think anything yet. We're not at that point. Don't let me down, Jim. Don't breathe a word."

"I won't."

Jim's mind raced: faulty materials used to build houses, Clyde Martin's death. Chain of evidence or coincidence? Plus, Pamela Holland's release from prison just before Clyde Martin's death – coincidence or another link in the chain?

Not being able to tell Pat what he had learned was especially hard. He told her most everything and valued her insight and experience. Most of all he valued her steady mind. His mind zigzagged all over the place. Others thought of him as steady, but he knew the truth: he was always trying ideas on for size and one size did not fit all.

Concentrate on Clyde Martin's death, he told himself. Leave the building collapse to law enforcement and the *Globe*, focus on where he, Jim Randall, retired judge acting on his own, could have the most impact. Having known George since childhood, Jim had a unique advantage, but George was cagey and would catch on if Jim probed too hard. He needed to spend more time with Miriam, the guardian of the realm, keeper of secrets. Get her to lower her formidable armor. Too great a challenge? Not if he turned on his charm. What charm? One advantage of having a reputation as a curmudgeon was that even a slight easing of attitude could make him seem charming; a half-smile, a grin. He was not above taking advantage of that.

Miriam wasn't buying his charm attack. No matter that Jim turned up at her office bright and early the next morning carrying flowers. "Your desk needs some color," he explained.

"I don't have a vase."

"Is George in? It would be like George to have a vase in his office. He was always prepared when we were kids."

"He's not here and won't be until noon. Dental appointment."

"Even with Clyde Martin's murder, George is thinking of his teeth?"

Miriam leaned forward conspiratorially. "Between you and me, Judge, he has problem teeth. Lots of pain. I don't blame him for taking care of his teeth and you shouldn't either."

"You two are close, aren't you?"

"We've worked together for twenty-five years. We know and respect each other but no one gets close to George, and no one wants to get close to me."

"Oh, I wouldn't say that. You don't give yourself enough credit. Does George have any quirks?"

That drew a laugh from Miriam, the first laugh Jim had ever heard from her. "Quirks? George doesn't have quirks."

"What's so funny?"

"Maybe you knew him once upon a time, but you don't know him now. The idea of George having quirks!"

"Maybe your quirks make up for his lack of them."

She went on full alert. "My quirks? I don't have quirks and don't think I don't see through your flowers."

"You're too smart for me."

Miriam eyed Jim. "Nice try, Judge. In my younger days, I might fall for whatever it is you're trying to pull, but for now, take your flowers and get out."

"Your desk really can use some color."

"I'm allergic. Get out, Judge."

Headline: Amateur Detective Strikes Out. Subhead: A Curmudgeon's Charm Fails To Please.

Plan B. Pamela again. He couldn't take anything she said for granted but untrustworthy people can accidentally reveal the truth. Worth a try.

A call to Sissy. May he come to Wellesley when both she and Pamela were there?

To drive from crowded mid-Cambridge to bucolic Wellesley was to pass through several time zones and cultures. He pulled up at Sissy's house marveling at the illusion that nothing bad could ever happen in this green and wealthy neighborhood. Sissy greeted him at the door.

"We're waiting for you, Judge. Pamela's in the living room."

"No, I'm here," Pamela said striding forward to stand beside Sissy in the hallway. "Catch the killer yet, Judge? I'm only joking."

"And I'm laughing inside, can't you tell?"

"Come in, Judge." Sissy stepped aside. A coffee pot and three cups awaited in the dining room. "I thought we could talk here."

When all three were seated and coffee poured, Sissy said, "The floor is yours, Judge." That elicited a grimace from Pamela.

Jim smiled. "What I want to know is what the two of you know about Holland Construction. As you both may have heard I spent time at the office and formed my own opinion about what goes on there, but I'd like to hear your takes on it. Do either of you think you know who killed Clyde Martin?"

Pamela stretched her hands palms down on the table. "I know who did it but I'm not going to tell you." She sat back, a smug look on her face.

Sissy didn't react well. "Stop it, Pamela! Why are you treating this as a joke?"

"Because the judge is such an easy mark," Pamela smiled. She seemed closer to sincere today. Not sincere but less insincere. "And why can't you ever call me Mom?"

Sissy shot back with no hesitation. "Number one, you may be my biological mother but you didn't raise me, my grandparents did, and number two, because you seem more child-like than mom-like and always have."

"Bicker another time you two," Jim said. "Pamela, did you glean anything from the prison grapevine about the murder at Holland Construction?"

Pamela was enjoying this. "Oh, good, you show me yours and I'll show you mine!"

"Okay, here's mine," Jim said. "I've learned that you, Pamela, became your disguises so long ago you can't remember who you truly are, and now you are desperate to recover your true self. Losing one's identity is terrifying, isn't it? You'd do anything to get it back. Maybe even kill."

Complete silence for a long moment, then, "If you're so smart, and *if* I were willing to kill, why would I kill Clyde Martin? Why not kill George, who divorced me? Huh? Tell me that."

"Maybe you came on to Clyde to get back at George, and Clyde wasn't interested. Maybe he came to seem like a stand-in for all the men who didn't fall for you." Jim continued without hesitation or pause. "I think you are a trusting and shy soul underneath your brazen exterior, Pamela. It's unlikely you killed anybody but you don't help your cause by playing the man-killer, if you catch my drift."

Pamela scrambled to recover her poise. "I need to spruce up my act."

"What I said about you is untrue?"

"No one's ever talked to me like that, until you, just now."

"But is it untrue?"

"I'm the wrong person to ask. And that's the truth."

Jim didn't need a gavel. He leaned forward. "Here's what I think. Much is at stake, and I don't want an innocent person to get caught in the gears of law enforcement. That means you, Pamela."

Jim could almost see Pamela changing facades until one fit her immediate needs. What emerged was a Pamela tempted but not quite ready to relax the face she showed to the world. After all, *femme fatale* was a useful disguise: women saw through it but men didn't dare.

Switch gears. Jim threw out a question. "Have either of you noticed a change in George since the murder?"

Sissy answered first. "He seems distraught. How would you feel?"

"Distraught for sure. Devastated, sickened, all of the above. I'm not pointing a finger, I'm asking a question."

Sissy's was the voice of reason. "He feels exactly like you'd feel, Judge. What are you getting at?"

"People who usually keep their feelings to themselves have been known to reveal themselves in extremis."

"Are you suggesting that George killed Clyde? Is *that* what you're suggesting?"

"Did he?"

"No, he did not. What do you think, Pamela?"

"I could see George killing someone but not with such brutality. George would kill with precision using the least amount of force possible. And he'd clean up afterwards. During our brief marriage, I was the slob, he was Mr. Clean." Pamela said this without posturing or mockery.

Pamela's opinion of people was suspect; she didn't know people, she used them. Stillness of soul is required to truly know someone, and stillness was a quality that Pamela lacked. But she might be onto something here, something about George that he, Jim, had not considered.

Jim drove back to gritty, brainy Cambridge wondering if childhood friendships had any utility when trying to understand a person as an adult. He was beginning to think not. Who the hell was George now?

For that matter, who the hell was he, Jim? Seventy was not just a number, it meant old age. Right? Or had the threshold of old age changed as people live longer? Order of business: solve this case, contemplate the meaning of turning seventy, give up and read the newspaper.

Golden Years? What idiot coined that phrase? His back and legs begged to differ. He wasn't deep into old age but he already knew that was absolute bunk, nonsense, balderdash and hogwash. Calm yourself, old man, don't let the ad men get you down.

He parked his car in his garage (a garage in densely packed Cambridge was much to be desired, rarely to be found) and went in through the backdoor.

5

Who killed Clyde Martin? Jim went into his living room mulling over what Pamela had said about George, that she could imagine him killing but killing with precision, without leaving a mess. The more Jim thought about that the more it resonated. Young George may have been Mr. Happy-Go-Lucky but he was also Mr. Clean.

If anyone could pry stray thoughts loose from George, it was George himself. So Jim thought. Worth a try.

He called George at home. "We need to catch up. How about a drink tomorrow?"

"I don't drink."

"Really? No matter. Bars have coffee, tea, any manner of non-alcoholic drinks."

Jim could hear George's chuckle, faint though it was. "No shit."

"When you were at my house for dinner, didn't you drink wine?"

"No, you poured some but I didn't drink it."

"I want to know you again, George. We used to get along so well. I don't think it was only because we were young. I'd like to get at least some of that back."

"A lot of water under the dam, my friend."

"Over the dam."

"Excuse me?"

"Water over the dam. Not under the dam. Water under the bridge, over the dam"

"Are you sure?"

"I'm not sure of anything."

"Makes two of us. Where should we meet?"

They met at a hotel bar on route 9 in Natick. It was anodyne in the extreme. Jim could imagine the supply catalog for hotel bar equipment: "Customers come to your bar to escape. Our standard-issue bars, bar stools, and mirrors will help them forget where they are."

Even the air smelled anodyne. Was there such a thing as bar air? Was it sold in the supply catalog?

George was already at the bar, tightly gripping his glass.

"There you are," Jim said taking the stool next to George.

George looked up. "Jim."

The bar didn't serve French wines so Jim settled for Italian. "What are you drinking?" he asked conversationally.

George shielded his glass. "Don't look."

"Beer? I thought you didn't drink?"

"Do I need a lawyer?"

Jim was taken aback by George's tone. "What's wrong, George? Why are you on edge?"

"Are you kidding? You didn't invite me here for old time's sake. We are here to interrogate me about Clyde Martin's murder. Am I right?"

"I'm retired, remember? I'm not on the bench any longer. Yes, I want to know who killed Clyde, but I have no official role. You want to know who killed him too. Maybe we can put our minds together."

George leaned back on his stool, hands raised in surrender. He looked as if he might cry. "I'm sorry, old friend. I hate that our friendship caught you up in this case. My life is a mess, and the messer-in-chief just got out of jail."

"Pamela?"

"Who else? She cannot stand things going smoothly. It implies there is life without her. Things are about to get messier."

For a moment, neither of them spoke. The hotel lounge was quiet and Jim could hear George's words ricocheting around the room. Loud. Louder than an ambulance siren, a police car.

Jim spoke first. "I've glimpsed the destructive force Pamela can be, but I wasn't ready to draw conclusions."

"Don't misunderstand me, Jim, I'm not saying – I repeat, *not* saying – that Pamela killed Clyde. I don't know who killed him, nor can I imagine anyone wanting to. Can you?"

"I don't know the people involved – including you now – well enough to have a clear idea. My mind is a blank slate as far as this murder is concerned."

George reply came after a split-second delay. "Jim, you never were a good liar." George's glass was empty. He signaled to the bartender for a refill. "Do you want another?" he asked Jim.

"I've barely touched what I have."

George tried without success to catch the bartender's attention. "There's almost no one in the bar except us. Why is this guy taking so long to refill my glass?"

"Easy, George. There's no rush."

"Yes, there is. Trust me, there is."

Jim drove home distracted. He was disturbed by the evening and tried to put it into a perspective that wouldn't reflect badly on his old friend. But try as he might, he kept coming back to the strong impression that his old friend was hiding something, a secret he longed to reveal but didn't dare.

Pat was in bed, reading, when he got home.

"How did it go?"

"I have a bad feeling. Either George killed Clyde Martin or knows who did, and/or he's guilty of the use of faulty materials in his buildings. He denies everything but more vehemently denies the murder. I hate to think of my childhood friend being implicated in either."

"Sounds like quite an evening." Pat was propped against three pillows. The reading lamp made half her face glow.

"Yes, it was. Quite an evening." While Jim undressed, he asked Pat, "What does one do when one suspects an old friend is guilty of a crime?"

"He gets in bed and shoves the old friend and crime out of his mind for the night."

Jim climbed into bed. "Good advice. Impossible to follow but good."

"Goodnight, Judge Randall."

"Goodnight, Judge Knowles."

*

Miriam was next. Ditch the charm. Go after her.

He showed up at Holland Construction without telling Miriam he was coming. She barely looked up from her desk. "Morning. What now?"

"I need to understand how Holland Construction is managed. You're the front line of the company. Tell me how you do your job."

That caught her off-guard. "How I do my job? It took me months to learn my job and years to master it, and you want me to explain it in a few words?"

"I'll settle for a few sentences."

"For what possible purpose?"

"I'm nosy. So tell me, what were your first steps when you got this job?"

Miriam stood and paced. "I don't like this. I don't like it at all. If George were here, he'd kick you out."

"George is away from the office a lot these days, it seems."

"He's earned his rest, Judge. My first steps? Dumb question. I made lists of potential suppliers and tradespeople, the way anybody would."

Jim nodded vigorously. "Good. Go on."

A proud woman, proud of what she had accomplished. "I worked well with Clyde. He assigned jobs, settled disputes, made the tough calls. I set up our bank accounts, kept a log of visitors and phone calls, managed the comings and goings. No one got past me. I could tell George was surprised by how short a time it took us to get the office running smoothly, but he shouldn't have been. Clyde was good at his job, and I am a capable woman, a very capable woman. I never let up. I take great pride in my work. I'll admit Clyde's murder knocked me off my stride, but I'm back to full speed. Satisfied?"

"Miriam, you need to relax. My oldest friend is involved, and I won't stop seeking answers until I learn the truth. I'm not out to get you, so lower your guard. Pretend I'm a trusted friend and tell me everything you know, even if it's only a guess."

Jim could see Miriam running that by her bullshit-detector, her mental Geiger-counter, checking its toxicity, its radioactivity, and to his relief, loosening a little.

"It's very hard for me to accept that George has done anything wrong. George is a good man." She paused to collect herself.

"Take your time."

"Lately there had been a palpable tension between George and Clyde. Neither would confirm but it was obvious. They had worked so well together for so long, I knew something had gone badly wrong. I told them I couldn't go on working with them if they didn't get along."

"The tension had been that bad, huh?"

"Just terrible. I've got pretty strong nerves but I couldn't continue doing my job if they were at each other's throats."

"Do you have any idea what the tension was about?"

She shook her head. "No idea. I once overheard Clyde yelling at George that he was surprised and disappointed by him, but I don't know what he was referring to."

"To your knowledge, was George thinking of selling Holland Construction?"

"If he was, I didn't know about it. George and I had a good working relationship. I admired him, did my best to make his workday happy. He treated me like his office wife, confiding his little aches and pains, his minor disappointments, but he didn't confide his business plans."

Jim was getting a better sense of her. She was all-business until she wasn't; devoted to George but even more so to her job. Jim had the sense that if she ever unlocked her emotions, she would dissolve into a puddle of tears. But he also sensed that she had forgotten where she hid the key.

"How well do you know the finances of the company?"

"I handle the payroll and tally the expenses, but we hire an outside firm to do the accounting."

"How well do you know the suppliers?"

"I talk to all of them."

"Any past problems with the materials they supplied?"

"None that I know of. Why do you ask? George prided himself for being hands-on, he loved talking with tradespeople, masons, carpenters, electricians, guys who built things. If there were problems, George would know. You want the truth? I think George would've been happier laying pipe or installing drywall than running a company."

"I didn't glimpse that about him when we were kids. Some kids are builders; they build with whatever is at hand: wooden blocks, Legos, you name it. Not George. He would rather climb trees."

Miriam frowned with worry. "Was he a happy child?"

"Always. Not a care in the world. You know him better now than I do. What do you think happened to change him?"

"Pamela happened to him. Between you and me, she ruined him. That's who she is. Not content to snare a man — that's only the first step — she has to ruin him, demonstrate to one and all her total control." Miriam narrowed her eyes. "Can't you tell that about her, Judge? You are more perceptive than most men. I'm surprised you don't see through her."

"Perhaps I do. Correct me if I'm wrong, Pamela was George's second wife?"

"Correct. His first wife died in her forties. He's confided in me his grief when she died. I was honored by his trust; George doesn't reveal his emotions often. By contrast, his marriage to Pamela was short and stormy. It ended when Pamela got pregnant by another man. George and his first wife didn't have kids, so at first George was thrilled about the baby, but when he learned he wasn't the father he was devastated and ended the marriage. George has never been the same since."

"Let me make sure I understand the family tree: Sissy is the child Pamela was carrying by another man while she and George were married?"

"Exactly. That's why George has such ambivalence about Sissy." Miriam stopped short, as if surprised to find herself talking so openly about her boss's personal life. "I've told you too much."

"Don't worry. Much of what you've told me, I already knew, but it's good to hear it from George's work wife."

"I'm his work wife? He told you that?" Her eyes widened.

"Yes. Anyway, seeing you two together in the office makes it obvious."

"I'm flattered." Miriam's hand flew to her cheek. Embarrassed by her emotion, she donned her work persona again: a cross between a prison guard and a schoolteacher cracking the knuckles of an unruly student. "George trusts you, Judge. I don't want George to know what I've told you." Sternly. "You owe me."

He smiled. "How do you want me to repay you?"

"Know your place from now on."

"You just smiled."

"I did not."

"I saw it with my own eyes, Miriam. The corners of your mouth turned up, ever so little but they did. Don't worry, I won't tell anyone. Your secret is safe with me."

Okay, he told himself on his way out, I now have a glimpse of where she hides the key.

*

Jim toyed with theories on his walk home (theories were his thing, give him a fact or two and a theory was sure to follow; sometimes just a hunch would do). What if Miriam killed Clyde? Jim had no clue what her motive would be but he toyed with the idea. Maybe unrequited love between an older woman (Miriam) and a younger man (Clyde)? 'Theories are my thing' would be the slogan on Jim's imaginary calling card.

How old was Miriam? Early sixties? White hair, permanent frown lines in her forehead, reading glasses which she rarely used and couldn't find when she needed them. In a way, she was timeless, without age, as if she had been born on the cusp of dotage.

Tony Rogers

He pushed Miriam as killer out of his mind so that he could enjoy dinner with Pat. The two of them went around the corner to Duck, Duck, Goose, their go-to restaurant. Jim ordered a glass of Côtes du Ventoux. The waiter was new.

"You're new here, aren't you?" Jim said with a question mark but meant as a statement of fact.

The young man smiled proudly. "Yes, two weeks."

Jim looked at Pat, then the waiter. "We live around the corner. We come here often."

"Yes. Bruce says you are among his best customers. No specials tonight, if you're wondering. You probably know the menu by heart, but here's one just in case."

"Thanks. Give us a second."

"Take your time. I'll bring your wine."

Jim absorbed the familiar dining room. He knew this about himself: he latched on to certain spaces – his courtroom; The Long Gone; Duck, Duck, Goose – as his safe places. Other people saw him as solid and dependable, if occasionally off-putting; he knew to the contrary that he was a wuss. He liked the word wuss.

Jim's wine arrived. He sipped it.

"Caution me, Pat."

"About what?"

"Mistaking cliches for clues."

"Cliches about what?"

"Women of a certain age who are married to their job."

"Like Miriam?"

"Yes, like Miriam. I imagine her alone and lonely, envious of those who are neither, falling in love with men she can't have. I'm probably full of it."

"Probably. I take it you're trying on for size the possibility that Miriam killed Clyde but can't understand what her motive would be. Maybe she loved him but couldn't have him, you are thinking?"

Jim lowered his head. "Shame on me for falling for the oldest of tropes, the lonely spinster, right?"

Pat replied, "It could be true but indeed shame on you if you base your thinking on a tired cliché about women."

Jim nodded. "That's why I said it out loud, so you could shoot it down. On the other hand, as you say, it could be true. Clichés are not automatically false."

The waiter appeared again. How do waitpeople sneak up on tables without being noticed? "Ready to order?" the eager young man smiled.

They both ordered cod. "Good boy," Pat said to Jim when the young man left. "I'm proud of you for skipping the steak."

Jim ignored her jibe. "Why is our waitperson so happy? He must be an out-of-towner."

"There, there. You'll feel better when you've had your wine."

The rest of the evening was uneventful. If you're with your loved one, uneventful can be the best kind of evening. As Jim and Pat walked around the corner to his townhouse, not in any particular hurry, for the millionth time he wondered if he and Pat should marry. But why? They had the degree of closeness which suited them. Sleeping dogs and old judges. His mind returned to Miriam. Is this what she lacked? This closeness? Had she twisted her thinking into knots so as to blame Clyde for not giving it to her?

"Jim!" It was Pat bringing him down to earth. "We're at your house. Do you have your keys?" He pulled them out of his pocket and showed them to her. "Of course I do."

"The next step is to unlock the door. You know, so we can go in."

"Say please."

"Please unlock the door so we can go in, Jim, dear."

"That's better." He turned the key and opened the door.

6

Ted Conover had been a young Assistant District Attorney when he first appeared in Jim's court. Twenty years later he still looked youthful, but time had given him a patina of wisdom.

He feigned annoyance when Jim entered his office. "What do you want this time?"

"To bother you. Are you going to offer me a seat?"

"Have a seat."

Jim sat. "George Holland was my childhood friend."

"I seem to remember you telling me that."

"Really? My memory is failing."

"Or mine is. Maybe you didn't tell me."

Jim nodded. "Anyway, I'm back in touch with George, and I'm worried about him. He's changed, and I would appreciate any heads-up you can give me that doesn't violate your ethics."

"This is about the alleged faulty construction materials?"

"Or anything else you find."

"That's intriguing. Do you think he killed Clyde Martin?"

"I hope and believe George is innocent of any wrongdoing, but it's a small company and there aren't many suspects."

"Normally, Jim, I would confide in you because I value your reactions and you don't leak. This time I can't for obvious reasons."

Jim nodded. "My objectivity is suspect."

"Correct. How's the world treating you otherwise, Jim?"

"Couldn't be better."

"You're lying."

"How can you tell?"

"You're much easier to read since you left the bench."

"Since I got old. I just turned seventy."

"Congrats. I didn't know."

"I am trying to ignore it."

"Your white hair and distracted air give you away. Hey, in honor of your old age I'll treat you next time we go to Ipsa Loquitur."

"Promise?"

"Promise. But only one round. One."

"When have you ever seen me drunk?"

"Never, except on power. Wielding a gavel, you were ruthless."

"Ouch. You don't mean that do you?"

Ted paused, hit rewind. "Sorry, Jim. Sorry. I was joking. You were always temperate and fair on the bench. None better."

Jim smiled. "Thank you, Ted. I don't know why I'm extra touchy these days."

"Let me count the ways. We'll continue this at Ipsa Loquitur. Again, sorry. Now I have work to do."

"Work? You have a job?"

"Don't push your luck, Old Friend, with the emphasis on old."

Jim walked home from Ted's office. It was a long walk but doable, even with his recalcitrant knees. Keep moving is the secret to life, he firmly believed. Keep moving.

Detouring via Beauty Shop Row took an extra ten minutes but was worth it. There was more life in the six blocks of beauty salons and barber shops than all of Back Bay, more life than on Brattle Street of Boston Brahmin fame. How to keep one's perspective when dealing with improbable crimes and unlikely criminals? Maybe by the end of his "career" as an amateur sleuth he'd have an answer to that. But for now he walked, movement being a good substitute for answers.

*

No solutions appeared to him overnight but plenty did by the time he was drinking his morning coffee at The Long Gone. Unfortunately none of the solutions related to Clyde Martin's murder or faulty construction materials, but he solved the world's pressing problems with ease.

The coffee shop was not crowded and Jim had his pick of tables. He chose a side table below one of the shoulder-high windows. The purpose of the window was to admit a little light, 'little' being the operative word because the window apparently had never been cleaned. Whatever light squeezed it's way through gave up in exhaustion before it reached Jim.

Of the trio of people who might know something about Clyde's murder – George, Miriam and, now that she had entered the picture, Pamela – he judged Pamela as the one most likely to accidentally reveal the truth. Blurt out something George or Miriam had said when she, Pamela, visited the office. He could imagine Miriam getting irritated and kicking Pamela out of the office. He could imagine George remembering old times with Pamela, when they were married, when they were making love, and saying more than he intended.

So he invited Pamela to have a drink with him that afternoon. He offered to meet her somewhere halfway between them.

They met in Newton in the cocktail longue of a chain hotel squeezed between sprawling apartment complexes on Highland Avenue, previously a street of useful shops and discount stores, now an uneasy mix of upscale apartments and eyesores.

The cocktail lounge (not a bar, mind you) was empty except for the two of them. They chose a booth near a large window overlooking a parking lot.

Pamela had toned down her look a little. Jim almost liked her. "I'm delighted you suggested this, Judge."

"Jim, please."

"No. Judge. I insist. Every time we meet you judge me. You don't hide it well."

"Once a judge, always a judge, I guess."

"What's it like, being paid to pass judgement on people? I think I'd love it."

"The idea of you being a judge amuses me."

"Why? Why does it amuse you?"

"Judge not, lest ye be judged."

"You think because of my exaggerated looks and shameless manner that I don't want people to know me? Au contraire. I desperately want people to know me. *Please* know me, that's what I'm pleading with my looks."

"Did you kill Clyde Martin?"

"Of course not. I wanted to fuck him, shatter his defenses, make him kneel and beg. Why would I kill him?"

"Because you couldn't have him. He eluded you."

She shook her head and grimaced. "Pathetic. Spoken like a man who has no clue about women."

"Apparently I need to brush up on my bombshell etiquette."

She squeezed Jim's forearm. "Bombshell etiquette! I love it!"

"If you didn't kill Clyde, who did?"

"George. George feels ill-used by life. His longtime first wife died and his second wife, that's me, cheated on him. I could see him killing Clyde out of envy for Clyde's stable life or resentment at how fiercely Miriam mothered him." Pamela lowered her eyes. In that instant, Jim understood Pamela's motives, she had explained them a moment before but until she coyly lowered her eyes, he hadn't fully understood that men were sport to her: a fisherwoman catching fish and throwing them back.

Pay attention Jim. She was saying something important. "Or maybe George and Clyde had a falling out over business secrets that Clyde knew and George didn't want revealed."

"Do you know something you're not telling me?"

She shook her head. "Forget I said that."

"No. You know something. Spill it."

"Well, hypothetically speaking, what if Holland Construction's business practices opened the company to criminal charges?"

"Go on."

She considered that for a moment. "I've said too much already."

"Finish what you started."

"Okay, so what if Holland Construction used shoddy materials in its buildings and Clyde was about to reveal the secret? Clyde knew everything that happened in that company. He opened up to me when I took an interest in him. I think he was grateful to have someone he could confide in."

"Why would he confide in you?"

"Men do. You can't understand that but they do. Especially the quiet ones." She paused. "I liked Clyde. He didn't pretend to be someone he wasn't. He was the genuine deal – a good guy – and in my experience they are hard to find."

"Pamela, you've been very helpful. I admit I was put off by your exaggerated manner at first, but you want to do the right thing, and not everyone does."

She squeezed Jim's forearm again. "I'm touched by that, I really am. But please don't let on to others what I'm really like or I'll have to find a new disguise."

"You can't just be yourself?"

"It doesn't work. Colorless doesn't work. Everyone needs a brand. Mine is over-the-top carnal with a little girl trapped inside. If men can't have me, they feel compelled to save me. It's complicated."

She paused in her confession, giving Jim time to absorb their anodyne surroundings. Recorded bar music played softly over a hidden speaker.

"Can I offer you another drink?" Jim said.

"No! I have to go. Now!" She jumped up and left suddenly. The same pattern as before. Fear she had revealed too much. Bolt. She was not as protected from prying minds as she looked.

That night, reading in bed with Pat, he reviewed his drink with Pamela.

"She is a fragile woman," he told Pat. "It took me a while to realize that, but now I do."

"Good for you. I could tell that understanding her had been on the tip of your mind since you met her, and I wondered when it would spill over into your thinking."

"You know what she said to me? What if Clyde knew about shortcuts the firm took that violated building codes. Like knowingly using shoddy materials. She said that."

Pat frowned. "Would that she were more reliable."

"I believe her in this case. She might bob and weave about herself and George, but she has no reason to lie about Holland Construction."

Pat grunted.

"Is that a yes-grunt, or a no-grunt?"

Before Pat could answer, Jim said excitedly, "You know what she said to me? Before she fled? 'Judge Randall, you're not the tight ass you seem to be.'" Jim laughed. "You're not the tight ass you seem to be!' Can you believe she said that to me?"

Pat shook her head. In the dim light it was hard to be sure. "Dear Jim. She got to you even as you were seeing through her disguise."

*

Pat was right, of course. He knew that even if he wasn't ready to admit it to her. Pamela was an accomplished actress and he was no more immune than the next guy. But at least he knew himself well enough to be able to push his feelings to one side now that he understood them, and concentrate on solving the crime.

Who killed Clyde Martin? He didn't think it was Pamela. She was too late to the game, so to speak, and he wasn't convinced by the motive he had conceived for her.

George? He had motive: Clyde knew secrets that could destroy the company. But Jim couldn't bring himself to believe that his childhood friend was capable of killing.

That left the longshot, Miriam.

But why would she kill Clyde?

Maybe she suspected Clyde was about to reveal the use of faulty materials, which would put Holland Construction out of business. She didn't want to lose her job or see the company George had built destroyed. That rang true.

But stabbing a man? Miriam? Sixty-something Miriam?

"Go to sleep, Jim." It was Pat.

"This murder is driving me crazy."

"No, you are driving yourself crazy. It's not your responsibility to solve this crime. Let Ted do it."

"I owe it to George."

"What if he's the killer? And what if you're the one who proves it? Will you be able to live with yourself?"

"Probably not. But I don't think he's our killer."

"I don't either, to tell the truth," Pat said. "I think it's Pamela. She gets out of prison, Clyde Martin dies. My guess is she had an affair with him before she went to prison and found he would have nothing to do with her now that she's out."

"You've been watching too many soap operas, Pat."

"I watch none, as you know."

"That was a metaphor, Pat. Here's what I think. I think we both need to chill."

"Why, Judge Randall, you used 'chill' like the young. I'm impressed."

"Keep up with the jargon and ye shall retain your youth, you've heard me say."

"You've never said that." She turned off her reading lamp with a resounding click.

"And former judge Patricia Knowles leaves her lover in limbo."

"Bailiff! Clear the courtroom."

*

He called Sissy first thing next morning. An idea had come to him in his sleep.

"We need to talk. Are you free this morning?" he asked.

As a free-lance editor and speech writer, she worked mostly from home. "That sounds ominous. Am I in trouble?"

"No. I just want to talk. I can come to your house."

"Pamela won't be here."

"Perfect. Tell me a time."

"It sounds like I have little choice."

"A time?"

"11. No, 11:30. I'll get sandwiches."

Sissy's comfortable, tastefully furnished living room made Jim want to confess his sins; nothing bad could happen to him in this room no matter how venial the sins. "Thanks for letting me interrupt your morning."

"Did I have a choice? Judge, you don't know how authoritative you sound when you say 'we need to talk'. A command by any other name."

"I hope I didn't scare you."

"You didn't, nor did I think I had a choice. I assume this is about Clyde's murder. I warn you not to expect too much from me. I have kept my distance from George and Holland Construction since I left home."

"Why?"

"Why what? Why did I think I didn't have a choice of whether to talk to you?"

"Because he wanted as little to do with me as possible. He deeply resented my mother getting pregnant by another man while they were married. I was that baby, ergo..."

"He hasn't been part of your life?"

"Why have you kept your distance from George and Holland Construction?"

"I rarely saw him and the few times I did, he cut the meetings as short as was humanly possible. All I remember from our meetings is his unease. I didn't get a sense of him otherwise."

Jim thought out loud. "I think your birth is what changed him from easy-going to bitter. Is your birth father alive?"

"No, he was killed by a drunk driver soon after I was born. I have no memory of him."

"I'm sorry. That was clumsy of me."

She waved that away. "Not your fault. I was too young to remember him or his death, so I've imagined a scenario to suit me. Robbing me of my father. So arbitrary, so unfair."

"Imagine what Clyde Martin was thinking when his assailant stabbed him."

"I've tried to put it out of my mind."

Jim had studied Sissy while they talked. He saw someone who didn't get in front of problems but held her own when pushed. To give himself time to think what that meant for his investigation, if anything, he changed the subject. "I've never met your husband."

"He's an ER doc. His hours are long."

"And high-pressure, I imagine. Has he done that for long?"

"A year. Before that, he was an internist." She stirred. "I picked up sandwiches for lunch. Are you hungry?"

"I could eat. And you're very nice to do that."

She got up. "Let's go to the diningroom."

"After you."

On the wall of the dining room was an oil painting of an august-looking man with reading glasses perched on his nose.

"Who is that formidable looking gentleman?" Jim pointed.

"An ancestor of my husband's. He invested his wealth wisely, then lost it all in the Great Depression."

"Sissy, you strike me as a wise woman, a woman who knows her own mind. You don't rush to conclusions, you withhold judgment until you are sure of yourself."

"I knew it."

"Knew what?" Jim said.

"Knew you were sizing me up."

"Yes, I was sizing you up in order to ask a question. From what you've told me, you may not want to answer the question. Is George capable of murder?"

She answered quickly. "Is George capable of murder? Yes. Did he kill Clyde Martin? No."

"What leads you to that conclusion?"

"Keep in mind that most of what I know about George comes from my mother, who as you have seen for yourself, is an unreliable witness. But one thing she said which rings true is that George is highly volatile underneath the placid surface. She had become afraid of him. If he hadn't left her, she would've left him. I could see him killing in a rage, but not committing cold, calculating murder."

"How did you turn out to be so level-headed with a mother like Pamela?"

"Who says I'm level-headed?"

"Correction. Seem to be."

"I wasn't going to let the circumstances of my birth drag me down. That was my mantra all the years I was growing up."

Jim lifted his sandwich but didn't eat it.

"You're checking out the sandwich. I'll save you the trouble. It's a BLT."

He took a bite. "It's good."

She laughed. "Like hell. Judge, you don't have to eat it."

"I'm not a very good actor."

"Oh, no, you are very good! Very, very good."

"I will appeal that judgement."

"Really, you don't have to eat the sandwich."

"I'll remove the bacon, okay?"

"Wait a minute." Sissy hurried to the kitchen and returned with an empty plate. "Here. For your bacon."

He smiled. "You should meet Pat someday. Pat Knowles. You two would hit it off."

"How did you get to know her?"

"We served on the court together. A woman with a backbone of steel and a well-concealed but very real funny bone. She keeps me from taking myself too seriously. We both had long marriages so know not to expect perfection, and the fact that we served for years together on the court meant we had realistic opinions of each other before we.... what is the current jargon?"

"Hooked up."

"Yes, before we hooked up. And we waited until we were no longer working together."

"You don't have to explain to me."

"I feel compelled to. I was thinking earlier that your living room feels like a confessional. And with that, I shall finish my sandwich and leave you in peace. I have no further sins to confess."

"What sins did you confess? I missed whatever they were."

Jim laughed. His full-blown laugh was hearty but rusty. I should laugh more often, he told himself before solemnity descended again.

He drove home through the shaded back streets of suburbia, futilely trying to pin down his feelings. He felt guilty for becoming so comfortable with Sissy, and his objectivity was already comprised by his long-ago friendship with George. How could he consider himself a good amateur sleuth if he got close to the people involved in a case?

He realized he wasn't paying attention to the road, so pulled over to the side in a neighborhood of large white colonials with big front yards separated by well-clipped bushes. It took a lot of wealth to create as convincing an illusion of invulnerability as this. Real life had ragged edges – beauty shop row versus upscale Wellesley. He preferred ragged edges, but it was a close call. He pulled away from the curb refreshed and ready to fight crime once more.

Pat was taken aback when he walked in the door. "Who are you?"

"Don't you recognize me? I'm the amateur sleuth, Jim Randall. At your service."

"I take it Sissy was helpful?"

"You may have a rival for my affections. Does that worry you?"

"Aren't you a little old for her?"

"Old?" Jim exclaimed. "I'm in my prime. Seventy is the new fifty."

"Yes, dear. Whatever you say."

He took off his coat and sat down beside her. "I'm getting too old for this."

"For chasing women?"

"I don't chase women, I don't have to. Who can blame them? I'm irresistible. Solving mysteries, that's what I'm getting too old for. Maybe I'll call it quits."

"You never officially started. You don't have to call it quits, just stop."

He stood up again. "Yes, I should quit. But I bet I won't. Now I'm going to the kitchen to get a glass of wine. Want any?"

"No, thanks."

He returned with a glass of red. "'I can't go on, I'll go on,' to quote Beckett."

"'A foolish consistency is the hobgobblin of little minds,' to quote Emerson."

"Cheers." Jim lifted his glass to Pat and drank.

7

First thing the next morning, Jim walked to the office of Holland Construction (get a feel for a place and person and the rest shall follow, crime was not that difficult to solve once the mind of the suspect was understood). Most of the buildings across the border in Somerville had once housed tool and die shops, auto repair shops, and cleaning companies, now many had been taken over by dental offices, dance studios, and day care centers. The low-slung buildings (none over two stories) retained their industrial charm. Actual things were once made here, real services offered, the buildings announced.

"Morning Miriam," Jim said as he entered the office.

She didn't look happy to see him. "You are getting on my nerves, Judge."

"A murder is more important than your nerves, Miriam. Don't you agree?"

She didn't answer the question, instead: "Are you here to see George?"

"I'm here to learn who killed Clyde."

She winced. "That he's gone still doesn't seem possible. I see him perching on the edge of my desk to ask a question. He trusted me to have the answers. Remembering his trust almost makes me cry."

Jim perched on the edge of her desk. "He sat like this?"

"Don't do that!" she snapped. "I mean it. Don't!"

"Sorry." He slid off the desk.

"You like breaking things, Judge, then looking for clues among the bits and pieces."

"You're smart, Miriam. Very smart."

Her eyes narrowed. "Cut the baloney, Judge."

"Oh, I wouldn't call it baloney. I'd call it buttering you up."

George emerged from the back offices. "Early in the morning for you to be up and about isn't it, Jim?"

"Sleuths never sleep, George."

"Catch Clyde's killer yet?"

"Not yet. Any new thoughts?"

George shook his head. "I haven't had a new thought for years. Tried and true, stick to the tried and true. We're done, Jim, you and I and people like us. Washed up. We can't go on and we can't go back. We're stuck where we are."

It struck Jim as out-of-character for George to wax existential while standing a few feet from where his right-hand man was murdered.

"I have to get back to work," George said, returning to form. "Miriam will get you anything you need."

Jim nodded in Miriam's direction. "She's always delighted to see me. Aren't you, Miriam?"

Miriam grimaced and growled, "Such a delight. I'm so lucky."

"But I've gotten what I need for now. I'll be going." As Jim turned to leave, Pamela barged through the front door with fury in her eyes. "I'll kill you, George! I mean it! I'll kill you!"

George seemed unfazed. "Calm down, Pamela. No need to kill me, I'm as good as dead."

She plopped down on one of the folding chairs. "What do you mean, as good as dead? Should I be worried about you?"

George seemed to realize she was actually worried, that it wasn't a show. His tone changed. "A figure of speech, Pamela. Nothing more. Why are you so upset?"

"I was questioned for hours and hours by the police."

"Hours and hours? Come on, Pamela," George said.

"Okay, half an hour!" She thrust both arms above her head, screaming, "I did nothing wrong yet they treated me like a criminal! You have the power to stop them, George. Just tell them the truth."

George looked embarrassed. "What truth? I don't know what you're talking about, Pamela. Don't listen to her, Jim."

Jim left them bickering in the office and walked home. He reviewed the day with Pat when they were reading in bed. Pat's response: "Pamela sounds like a woman who overreacts to every slight, real or imagined. Who takes every pinprick and sideways glance personally. Consider this: Pamela comes on to Clyde, Clyde rejects her advances, Pamela loses control."

When Jim had no immediate response, Pat prompted him. "What are you thinking, Jim?"

"Nothing."

"Not true, what I said triggered something in your mind. What exactly?"

"I think the scenario you imagined could lead to Pamela exacting some sort of revenge but not murder. I don't detect that in her."

"My, my. Et tu, Judge Randall?"

"What do you mean by that?"

"Not a thing."

"No, what do you mean?"

"Nothing I haven't said before."

"You don't understand Pamela. Pamela lacks impulse control but isn't crazy. She views seduction and rejection as part of the big game of life and wouldn't kill over it. And now I put my amateur tool kit away for the night." He switched off his bedside lamp.

"Have you excluded Miriam as a suspect?"

"I haven't excluded anybody, I'm still collecting information. But it's hard for me to imagine the mother hen of the office killing one of her chicks. Besides, I'm beginning to appreciate Miriam. She's has gentleness beneath the steel. The growl and scowl are her suit of armor."

Pat paused before replying, "And amateur sleuth Randall watches objectivity fly out the window. First about Pamela, now Miriam. And you've never had objectivity regarding George."

Jim turned onto his side, his preferred sleeping position. "Objectivity is not everything. Objectivity is essential to identifying whodunnit, but subjectivity is essential to discovering whydunnit. And once the 'why' is known, the 'who' can be glaringly obvious. So saith the oracle of Mid-

Cambridge as his final pronouncement for the night." He closed his eyes and pretended to snore.

Not that many hours later he was drinking his first cup of morning coffee in the kitchen when the phone rang.

It was Ted Conover telling him that the offices of Holland Contracting had been broken into during the night. "The night watchman hired by the business owners to patrol the neighborhood spotted an unmarked black van without its lights on leaving the area around 2 a.m. The watchman alerted the police."

"Anybody hurt?"

"No. No one was in the office."

"Any other businesses broken into?"

"None that we know as of yet, but it's still early."

Jim checked the kitchen clock. 7:30 a.m. "What the hell are you doing at work this early in the morning, Ted?"

"I'm still at home. I got a call from my office reporting the break-in."

"Do you know what the thief or thieves were after?"

"Holland Construction doesn't keep a lot of cash in the office. We're thinking the theft had to do with lawsuits against the company. Maybe the thief sought records to bolster its case that Holland Construction used substandard materials it knew might eventually fail."

Pat had come downstairs while Jim was on the phone. "I'm putting my money on the break-in having to do with Clyde Martin's death," she said when Jim got off the phone. "To get rid of evidence, perhaps."

"That may be true. You have more objectivity about this case than I do."

George called while Jim was pouring himself a second cup of coffee.

"Jim, I've got a problem."

"Your offices were broken into."

"How did you know?"

"It doesn't matter. Is everyone okay?""

"No one was in the office at the time. We're fine."

"Good. Good. You must be shaken."

"I am."

"George, before we proceed, I have to ask; did you know faulty materials were being used in your buildings?"

"I'm surprised you could ask that of me, your childhood friend. No, Jim, I'm more baffled and upset than anyone by the accusations, and now our offices were ransacked. What the hell's going on?"

"I was hoping you could tell me."

"Not a clue."

"Let's talk this through at The Long Gone. I do some of my best thinking there."

"Do I need my attorney?" Slight pause. "That was a joke."

Jim answered seriously. "No, you don't need your attorney but hold that thought."

The Long Gone smelled of fresh coffee and early risers the next morning. George and Jim had a four-person table to themselves. No one was close enough to overhear.

George looked wide awake and eager to talk.

"This whole thing has upset me like nothing before," he began as soon as he sat down. "I know how it looks. But you don't believe I had anything to do with Clyde's tragic death or the materials scandal, do you?"

"Clyde's death, no. The materials scandal, maybe."

George was deeply hurt. "My oldest friend. How could you think that of me?"

Jim had sat alone in The Long Gone many times but had never felt as alone as he did now sitting with George. He didn't believe his friend capable of murder, but cutting corners to maximize profit? George was human.

"Better men than you and I have succumbed to the profit motive, George."

"Innocent until proven guilty, Jim." George surveyed the handful of customers at other tables. "Does it get busier than this?"

"Much busier. This is takeout coffee time. Later in the day students with their laptops settle in."

Jim looked at his friend. George was lost in thought. Jim let him think.

When George broke his silence, the sound was explosive, as if feelings long locked inside had burst through steel barriers. "You expect me to crack, don't you? Invite me here and let me sit and stew until I confess, even if I didn't do anything. That's what you're hoping for, right?"

"I have no expectations."

George's voice grew tighter and tighter. "You'd settle for a false confession, wouldn't you? Well, I won't give you the pleasure, Jim. You are a false friend and I regret ever contacting you!"

"Don't say that, George."

George jumped to his feet with an anger that startled Jim. "Screw you."

"Sit down, George." Too late. George was out the door.

Jim left The Long Gone. Standing on the sidewalk in front of the coffee shop, he called Pat.

"Pat, I think I've permanently alienated George. I need to go to Vermont. Want to come?"

"Do I have a choice in the matter?"

"Of course you do, but I need to clear my head."

"I'm worried about you, Jim. Yes, I'll come with you."

Never had Jim driven to his Vermont house feeling so conflicted. He drove faster than usual, alarming Pat. "Jim?"

"I ignored my own advice to stay out of this case. Why didn't I listen to me?"

"Because it's harder to take your own advice than someone else's."

The Vermont house was north of Brattleboro, overlooking the Connecticut River which marks the border between Vermont and New Hampshire. The familiar odor of stale air and mouse droppings leapt up to greet them when Jim opened the front door. The first thing Jim always did when he entered the house was gaze out the long windows in the living room at the river valley. Today the river itself was hidden by a thin layer of mist. Heraclitus said that one can never step in the same river twice; nor, according to Jim Randall, can one see the same river twice.

"I needed this," Jim said, turning away from the window.

"The place needs a good cleaning," Pat said.

"Tomorrow, after we settle in. Tonight we go out to eat and forget all else."

The options ranged from an all-day diner to a white tablecloth restaurant at a nearby inn. They chose the restaurant. The food was not special but the experience was reliably reassuring.

The waiter recognized them. "Haven't seen you for awhile."

"Haven't been here for awhile."

"Welcome back."

Pat admonished Jim once the waiter had gone. "Jim, you sounded abrupt."

"I thought I sounded jocular."

"You still don't know how you come across to others."

"I guess I'll never learn."

"There. Abrupt again."

Pat ordered a glass of white wine, Jim red, and they toasted each other. They didn't talk about Clyde Martin's death until after they ordered.

"According to security tapes and the neighborhood night watchman, Miriam was last to leave the offices the night of Clyde's murder. Pamela stopped by the office briefly and left by herself, George was next to leave and Miriam left last. Clyde was never seen leaving. The autopsy puts the time of his death between 5 and 9. Miriam is the most likely suspect. The question remains, whydunit?" Jim offered the opinion as to a jury. He was mildly surprised when Pat was the person who answered, not a jury forewoman.

"Don't torture yourself, Jim. Let Ted and the police handle this."

"I can't do that. I owe it to George."

"Which is exactly why you should stay out of it."

"Too late for that now. Like it or not, I'm all in."

"You're usually so levelheaded. I worry that you've lost your equilibrium."

"Are you saying you think George is guilty?"

"I didn't say that. I said you aren't being levelheaded."

"Old friends owe each other something."

"Lets drop it for the night."

The drive to Jim's house up and over the darkened hills of Vermont was usually soothing but not tonight. Tonight the hills felt eerie, sinister. He was relieved when they arrived home safely.

As Jim unlocked the door, he offered this: "George didn't kill Clyde, nor did Pamela."

"That leaves Miriam."

"Correct. But my God, what an unlikely killer!"

"Will you be able to put this aside long enough to get some sleep?" Pat asked.

"Probably not."

They stayed for a second day, an anxious day which neither of them enjoyed, at which point they gave up and drove home. Jim's first call when they got back to Cambridge was to Ted Conover.

"I'm back."

"I didn't know you were away."

"I was, but now I'm back."

"In answer to the question you are about to ask. No, we haven't solved the murder yet nor have we established with certainty who instigated the construction materials scam. We think your friend George did the latter and that Clyde Martin oversaw the operation once it was underway."

"Not Miriam Summers?"

"No, she ordered the supplies, but Clyde told her what to order and from whom. Our working hypothesis is that George Holland wrote the score, Clyde Martin conducted the orchestra, and Miriam Summers was the concertmaster."

"How are you proceeding?"

"With all deliberate speed."

"ETA?"

"Unknown. Days if we're lucky, any moment if we strike gold."

"Maybe you and I will reach eureka at the same time. Wouldn't that be something, Ted? I can see a cosmic explosion of some sort, a black hole event."

"You're chuckling, aren't you? I can hear it over the phone."

"Chucking? I never chuckle. Chortle occasionally, but never chuckle."

"Jim, when we close this case, we shall chortle in unison at Ipsa Loquitur."

He wondered if Sasha at the *Boston Globe* had any new info. He invited her for coffee at The Long Gone.

She hurried in the next morning as if she owned the place but didn't want to be noticed. It was always good to see her. She took a seat across from Jim

"Hey," she said, elbows on the table.

"Hey, yourself."

"What's wrong, Jim?"

"Why do you think something's wrong?"

"Because you look vexed. Where have you been?"

"Vermont."

"Siberia."

"Now Sasha, you are not *that* much of a city person."

"I wither and die when I'm out of the city."

"We both know that's not true."

"What's new at Holland Construction?" she said, leaning closer.

"That's what I wanted to ask you. Any new leads?"

She shook her head. "Our paper's gotten a ton of drivel from the usual conspiracy theorists. My favorite is that Holland Construction is the North American listening post for extraterrestrials. Nothing credible. Sorry."

Jim was discouraged. Even a walk on Beauty Shop Row did nothing to cheer him up. Maybe he should get his eyebrows threaded for a change of pace.

He decided to continue walking across the Longfellow Bridge to Pat's. She had a book club meeting that morning but he had a key. Which he used to enter after he climbed Beacon Hill. First time he had climbed the steep hill since he turned seventy. He was delighted to find that his legs still carried him. He was more winded than usual but he could live with that. Damn, Jim, you're really spooked by old age, aren't you?

Pat's apartment felt as much like home as his townhouse. He made himself coffee in the kitchen and carried it to the living room.

Thinking about the murder, he got furious with himself. What if George *is* guilty? Was he, Jim Randall, former judge of the Massachusetts Superior Court, amateur sleuth, irascible senior citizen, too stubborn to accept that loyalty was not always a virtue? What kind of a sleuth was he? Amateur was too kind, incompetent was more like it.

The front door opened. Pat was startled when she saw him. "I didn't know you were here."

"Spur of the moment thing." He rose to his feet. "My self-esteem is crashing, Pat."

"Tell me what's happened."

"George happened. I've been a lousy detective."

She came to him and gripped his arm. "No one bats a thousand. In this case you are down on yourself because of loyalty to an old friend which usually is a good thing."

"It isn't when you're trying to solve a murder."

"It's not too late to leave this case to others, Jim. A lot of people are working on this, people whose job it is. Leave it to them."

"I'm taking this case too personally, aren't I?"

"Yes, you are, because George is involved."

It felt good to be understood. At the end of the day that's all any of us want. He was a good judge, a middling amateur detective, a sometimes loyal friend, and an apprentice senior citizen. Perfection was neither called for nor possible. Don't despair because you're imperfect.

He faced a choice. Embrace the case without emotional reservation or abandon it altogether. No halfway measures. Before you choose, get to know your childhood friend George as he is now, not as he and you were as children. Of course, when Jim had tried before, George stormed off, but what the hell.

George on the phone sounded wary, tentative. "Just the two of us? For a weekend?"

"It's peaceful and beautiful. We'll be able to relax, George. A weekend in Vermont will do us both good."

"How can I relax? I'm under suspicion for murder."

"We'll remember old times for a weekend, forget the present."

"My job is 24-7, Jim."

"Miriam can handle things for a few days. And there's always the telephone."

"You have telephone service that far north?"

"Spotty, but yes, we do."

"Lighten up, Jim, I was joking."

"I'll pick you up tomorrow morning at 9, okay?"

"I suppose."

8

When they crossed the Vermont line, Jim felt a change in air pressure. Was it internal or external air pressure? There was no pop in his ears as in a descending plane, just a gentle decompression, a 'relax all ye who enter here' sort of feeling. He should have proposed this trip sooner.

George felt the change too. Jim was sure and was startled to be sure. This wasn't the same George he had grown up with, so how could Jim know what he felt? But he was sure he could.

He showed George around his place first thing. Given the small size of the house, it didn't take long.

"The bedrooms are at the end of the hall. Mine is to the right, yours to the left."

George seemed impressed. Especially when they were in the living room and Jim pointed out the window to the river valley. At this hour, the river was eclipsed by the sun. "That's the Connecticut River."

"Where?" George said.

"Underneath the sun's glare. No criminal wears better disguises than the Connecticut River."

George didn't take Jim's bait. "Beautiful, truly beautiful. I can see why you like this place. I'm a city person myself, but I can see why you like it."

"I propose we eat in one night, but tonight I'll treat you to dinner at my favorite inn."

"We're going back on Monday?" George sounded nervous.

"That's the plan. We can stay longer if you want. That's your call."

George tried to sound lighthearted. "So I'm not being held hostage?"

"Oh, you are. Ball and chain."

George chuckled. "How about a beer?"

Jim fetched a Long Trail IPA from the kitchen.

"You're not having one?" George said.

"I'm a wine person."

"What's stopping you from having a glass of wine now?"

"Self-discipline."

George looked confused. Jim tried to explain.

"I don't trust my judgement when I've had a glass or two at this hour. Later, at dinner, I shall indulge."

"Out of curiosity, won't your friend Ted think you're hiding me?"

"Ted Conover? The ADA? I let him know where I was taking you and why, and told him I would accept full responsibility for bringing you back when he wants to talk to you."

George sat on the sofa and drank his IPA. From the sofa, one could see the sky above the river. The water made its presence known by causing the sky above it to shimmer.

"I didn't do it, Jim."

"It?"

"I'm not a killer, nor am I naive. I accepted your invitation to come to Vermont because I know you are relentless, that you won't stop until you have your answers, and I want to get in front of whatever you're going to ask."

"I invited you here because I feel hampered by not knowing you well as an adult," Jim said.

"I'm not that different. Less trusting, more cynical perhaps, but still the George you knew. I'm not a killer or a crook."

George took a walk by himself before dinner. Jim took a nap.

"Where did you walk?" Jim asked as they drove to dinner.

"Along the ridge. Nice view."

Jim nodded. "I love it here. My late wife and I bought the house when we worked in state government in Montpelier, and I return often."

"What was she like?"

"Joyce?"

"Your late wife, yes."

"We had a good marriage – dissimilar personalities but devoted to each other. But we never bonded in the ways our years on the bench bonded Pat and me. Pat and I don't ask of each other what the other can't give."

"Did you and Joyce have kids?"

"No. We tried but it was not to be."

"Sissy and I have never been close," George said regretfully. "I rarely saw her after I divorced Pamela. My bad." George turned away from Jim and headed towards his room. "Enough for now. We can talk more over dinner."

It was still light when they drove to the inn. "It's nice up here," George said.

"You said that before."

"Well, it's true. I don't get up to the country often enough. I should take advantage of what the region has to offer."

"What do you like to do in your downtime?"

"What downtime? A small business is all consuming. But it's worth it; I take pride in Holland Contracting being acknowledged as one of the best in the greater Boston area."

Jim was watching the road intently.

George studied him for a few seconds. "Are you taking my words seriously?"

"Forgive me if I seem distracted."

They were approaching the inn. Jim said, "It'll be dark when we drive back. A time for ghosts and goblins. I hope you're not easily spooked."

"What's that supposed to mean? I detect multiple layers of meaning in everything you say since Clyde was murdered."

"I'm listening to you on several levels, old and new, hoping to recapture some of our old friendship before present-day circumstances intrude."

George smiled after a millisecond time delay. "That sounds like a grownup version of the Jim I knew as a kid. You were never content with surfaces, always wanted to know what's beneath."

Jim nodded. "Problem is, I don't know you well enough now to know if I'm seeing the river or the haze."

George shook his head. "I'm not worth the effort, Jim. Don't waste your time."

Jim patted George's shoulder as they stepped over the threshold of the restaurant. "You seem too down on yourself to decide whether you're worth my time. I predict you'll like this restaurant. Let's see if I'm right. Watch your step."

The inn couldn't be more New England-y if it tried. Sprawling white colonial with a wraparound front porch. The restaurant was in the rear of the inn. The maître-d remembered Jim. "Welcome back, Judge. Where's Judge Knowles?"

"Back in Boston. This is my childhood friend, George Holland."

The maître-d did a little bow. "Welcome to you both. I shall do everything possible to make your evening pleasant." He showed them to a window table. "Can I get you started with drinks while you make up your minds about dinner?"

George ordered a bourbon, Jim his usual French red.

George scanned the menu. "What's good here?"

"Just about everything. I'm going to have the cod."

"I'm not a fish person."

"Neither am I, but I'm increasingly conscious of my health." Jim closed his menu and waited for the wine. What had caused George to sound so pessimistic, to say he wasn't worth it? What did he mean by that? Did it reflect the pessimism of old age, or was he confessing to a crime? Jim's initial impulse was to simply ask, "You said you weren't worth it. What did you mean by that, George?" Jim usually preferred the direct approach but had learned that sometimes he got the best result when he didn't lead the witness.

George was talking about his father. "Before he died my father routinely belittled me. Never hit me but left indelible scars."

"You never told me this."

"I thought it was my fault, and after Dad died, I felt guilty whenever I thought of telling you. And then, of course, Mom and I moved away, and you and I lost touch."

"Why did we lose touch?" Jim asked. "We could have stayed in touch."

George shook his head. "I don't know. Life takes over."

"And here we are. Your right-hand man dead and your company's future in question."

"I'm not guilty, I don't know who killed Clyde nor did I know we were building buildings that might collapse." Pause. "You believe me, don't you, Jim?"

"I can't say I do, George. I'd like to."

"You said once before you didn't think I killed Clyde, is that still true? Please at least tell me that?"

"Are ready to confess to knowingly using shoddy materials in your buildings? Are you telling me that?"

"I'm tired, Jim, tired of looking over my shoulder, tired of lying."

"Then tell me the truth."

George, under his breath, "Yes."

"Yes, what?"

"I did what you said I did."

"You risked using materials you knew might fail?"

"Not at first, and not always."

Jim got mad. "Dammit, George! No qualifications or excuses. Did you sometimes use materials you knew might fail?"

"Yes."

"Was that so hard?"

"Yes, it was. But I didn't kill Clyde."

"Now I believe you. What's your guess who did?"

"Pamela. She doesn't possess the normal guard rails. She flirted with Clyde as soon as she got out of prison. She's not subtle. I don't know if she had a thing for Clyde before she went to prison, or whether she hoped to use him to send a message to me, the man who divorced her. I can envision her impulsively killing Clyde if he didn't give her what she wanted. She's a spoiled, bitter woman."

"Which could be second degree homicide instead of first if that's what happened."

"It wasn't me, Jim, that's the only thing I'm sure of. Do you believe me?"

"Yes, now I do. I'll set up a meeting with my friend, Ted Conover, in the DA's office, to talk about the construction fraud. Don't you dare backtrack or lie, George. I've known Ted a long time and he'll take into consideration all the circumstances surrounding what you did as long as you're straight with him."

"What circumstances? I didn't kill Clyde, but I did cheat our customers."

"Yes, but you built a successful business from scratch, a small contracting company in a field of mega-builders, a man who saw a way to increase profits and succumbed to temptation, etc., etc. I'm not saying Ted will look the other way, but he will weigh the good with the bad. The fact that you confessed to me will work in your favor, both with Ted and the jury."

"You think it will go to trial?"

"Yes, I do. Ted's got a heart but he's by-the-book. You broke the law. Ergo, raise your right hand and repeat after me...."

Jim and George drove home from the inn in silence. The night cooperated. The darkness felt benign. The hills harbored no secrets.

When they got back to the house, the house felt emptier than usual. George seemed unsteady when he walked down the hall to the bathroom.

"Are you okay?" Jim asked when George returned to the living room.

"Define okay. My conscience is relieved, but I am no longer sure of who I am. How about a nightcap?"

"You've had enough, George. You need sleep. You'll wake up during the night feeling terrible and not be able to get back to sleep. I hope you then realize you have partially set things right by leveling with me. Goodnight, George."

"Goodnight. Jim. Do you think I'll be locked up while I await trial?"

"I doubt it. I think I can persuade Ted you're not a flight risk."

"Thank you."

Jim texted Pat after he climbed into bed –

A good day. I'm too exhausted to give you a play-
by-play. Tell you more tomorrow. Goodnight.

He barely slept. Even when he drifted off, he listened for George. Halfway through the night, he crept into the living room and saw George asleep on the sofa with silly putty arms and legs.

Jim awoke at first light. Quietly, he checked to see if George had gone to his bedroom. He hadn't. He was still on the sofa. As far as Jim could tell he hadn't moved during the night. Jim gently touched his shoulder to see if he was alive. George startled awake.

"Sorry, didn't mean to wake you. Wanted to see if you were still alive."

George sat up. "What time is it?"

"6 in the morning."

"I must have fallen asleep on the sofa."

"You needed the sleep. Want coffee?"

George rubbed his face back to life. "Coffee would be good."

In the kitchen, Jim texted Pat –

> George just woke up. Quite a night.
> Accomplished its purpose.

Pat's reply was instantaneous –

> I assume you're fine? No scars?

Jim –

> None that are visible.

Pat –

> When are you boys coming back?

Jim –

Soon. Very soon.

Jim took the coffee into the living room. George had gone to the bathroom. Jim went to the windows and looked at the early-morning river. In the low-slanting sun, he couldn't tell if its surface was rippled or smooth. He heard the toilet flush and a few seconds later, George appeared in the living room. He came to stand beside Jim.

"What are you looking at so intently?" he asked.

"The Connecticut River."

"I still don't see it."

"Beneath the haze."

"Is that one of your metaphors?"

"I'm going to drive down to the general store to get doughnuts and muffins. Want to come?" Jim asked.

"Let's go."

As they drove down the hill, Jim said, "We could walk down, but then we'd have to walk back up."

"God forbid," George said.

"What do you do to keep in shape?"

George was more than a few pounds overweight. "As little as possible."

The general store was Jim's go-to place for all things he forgot to get in town. It had donuts and muffins in the morning, always a basket of locally-baked breads, and shelves and shelves of canned and dry goods. And of course, hot coffee all day, regular and decaf.

Jim studied the muffins. He chose mixed berry. George carefully chose two glazed donuts.

They ate at the window stools. "We'll go to the house to use the bathroom, then drive back to Cambridge. Okay?" Jim said.

George nodded. "Are you planning to stop at the DA's office before we go to your house?"

"No. I'll call him on the way and see how he wants to handle it. I imagine he'll set a time for you to turn yourself in. I'll come with you, of course."

"Jim, I'm grateful. To the extent I have any dignity left, it's because of the way you've handled this."

"Admit it, George. You had this in mind when you and I became childhood friends. Right?"

"Of course. You think I actually liked you?"

9

They said little on the drive back to Cambridge, and what little they said was small talk: comments on the towns they drove through, 'I see why you like it up here', that sort of thing. The mood in the car was subdued compared to their drive to Vermont. Both had been wary on the drive up; on the drive back, both were weary.

As they neared Boston, Jim called Ted. He got his voicemail.

"Ted, it's Jim Randall. My friend George Holland is ready to make a partial confession. I'll come with him. Let me know what time."

Jim turned to George. "Okay?"

George nodded. "Will you drop me off at Sissy's? I want to explain to her what's about to happen. I promise I won't disappear."

"Don't. If you do, you'll be caught and you'll be in worse trouble."

"Jim, we're past the point of wondering whether you can trust me. I just need to be with Sissy one more time before I turn myself in."

"Okay."

They pulled up at Sissy's house. Almost before they came to a halt, George slid out of the car. "Let me know what time we meet with Ted."

Jim called Ted from his townhouse but did little the rest of the day. When Pat came to Jim's house before dinner, she found him slumped in a living room chair. She uttered a worried cry.

Jim stirred. "I'm alive. Just recovering from the last few days. George is turning himself in tomorrow. Ted is expecting us."

Pat approached his chair. "Poor Jim. This will haunt you for years but you did the right thing."

"I know, but geez...nothing in life prepared me for this. Turning in a friend is not taught in law school." Jim sat up as straight as he could. "I have to pull myself together."

"Jim, you being involved will ensure that George is treated with the utmost fairness."

"Stop trying to make me feel better. You can't."

"Am I correct that George confessed to business fraud but not the murder?"

"Correct. Once George and I meet with Ted, I will resume searching for the identity of Clyde's killer."

"Remember, Jim, finding the answer doesn't rest solely on your shoulders."

"I know, I know. Let's drop this and call Bruce. If I ever needed the solace of a good meal in a safe place, it's tonight."

Bruce, of course, had a table for them at Duck, Duck, Goose. Jim had the steak knowing it was bad for him. The hell with health for one night.

"Don't rub it in," Jim said when he caught Pat looking at him.

"Rub what in?"

"One steak won't kill me."

"I didn't say it would."

"But that's what you were thinking. 'Jim shouldn't eat steak.' I know you."

"Yes, you do and yes, I was."

Jim smiled. It felt good to smile. He hoped Ted would be sympathetic to George when they met.

*

George met Jim at the DA's office the next morning. They had to wait in the outer office for ten minutes before Ted could see them. Neither of them spoke.

When Ted emerged from his office, he looked even more business-like than usual. "Sorry to keep you waiting. I've invited one of my younger attorneys to join us. Come this way."

Ted ushered them to his office, an office which Jim knew well – on the wall behind Ted's desk, the faded painting of a sailboat leaning into the wind; on the desk, photos of Ted's two boys, both of whom were now college graduates, one from Princeton, one from Dartmouth. Each time Jim saw the photos, he mused that he would know the world was about to end when Ted moved either of the photos a millimeter.

Ted gestured to a preppie-looking young man sitting by the wall. "Gentlemen, this is Horace Swain. He's here to serve as a witness. Please be aware that this meeting is being recorded." Ted sat down behind his desk. "Jim, the meeting is yours."

"Ted, thanks for agreeing to meet with us on such short notice. For the record, I am Judge Jim Randall, formerly of the Massachusetts Superior Court, and with me is George

Holland, founder and president of Holland Construction of Somerville, Massachusetts, a friend of mine from childhood."

The color drained from George's face as Jim turned to him and said, "George?"

George began haltingly. "I'm here to confess to a long-standing scheme to defraud our customers by buying materials not adequate for the job while charging top prices." George stopped to clear his throat. Then tumbled out the whole story, how the fraud started, why it continued, who was in charge. "Clyde Martin ran the scheme on a day-by-day basis but the original idea was mine and I approved everything Clyde did. I take full responsibility."

"Did any of your buildings collapse, Mr. Holland?"

"No. I lucked out."

"As you know, there was a recent incident where a balcony built by another contractor collapsed, killing a teenager."

"I know. That's part of the reason I'm confessing today. It's only a matter of time before that happens to one of mine, and I don't want that on my conscience."

Ted let George's words hang in the air. After a silent minute, Ted asked, "Anything you wish to add, Mr. Holland?"

George could barely croak. "No."

"Okay. I'll arrange for an arraignment as soon as possible. You give your word that you will appear for the arraignment, Mr. Holland?"

"You have my word."

Jim spoke. "And I'll make sure he does. He knows what he did was wrong and is ready to atone for it."

Jim went to Pat's apartment on Beacon Hill for the night. He felt out-of-place, his thinking muddled, as if he had passed through several time zones on a very long flight.

"How did the meeting with Ted go?" Pat asked.

"No surprises. George will be arraigned Monday morning."

"You'll accompany him to his arraignment?"

Jim nodded. "Of course. I think what's about to happen is just hitting him. By the end of our meeting with Ted, George looked as if he were already wearing a prison uniform."

Pat and Jim were sitting in her living room. A glass of wine perched on the arm of Jim's chair. "I felt like a traitor, Pat. First time in my life I've felt like a traitor for doing my legal duty." Jim attempted a wry smile.

"Does George face jail time?"

"That's my guess. If I know Ted he'll ask for a sentence severe enough to send a clear message but not severe enough to shatter George. It's hard to tell."

"What are you going to do now that half the mystery has been solved? As if I didn't know."

"Solve Clyde Martin's murder."

"You can't leave that to Ted? You've already done enough."

"I know."

"That's not going to stop you, is it?"

"Not a chance."

"Where are you going to start?"

"I want to hang out in Miriam's office again."

*

Miriam was not happy to see him. He arrived as she was opening the office.

"Haven't you done enough harm already, Judge?"

"Just getting started. I take it you heard about George?"

"Yes. Directly from George. He stopped by to tell me in person." Tears came to Miriam's eyes. "George is such a good man."

"Then I assume you know why I'm here."

"You haven't irritated me enough so you're back to finish the job."

"Correct." Jim eyed the folding chairs. "By now you know my method. I'll just sit here and observe for as long as it takes."

"What if I call the police and have you thrown out?"

"I was a judge with a good reputation with the police. Go ahead and call them."

Miriam sighed. "You might as well sit. It will be a waste of your time, but apparently you have time to waste."

Jim picked one of the folding chairs. "You need better chairs."

"I don't want people getting comfortable. Do your business and get out, the chairs say, as do I."

During the course of the morning several tradespeople checked in but otherwise the office was quiet. Miriam kept busy, barely acknowledging most of the tradespeople, trading quips with the others.

"Business seems slower than usual," Jim broke the silence midway through the morning.

"That should make you happy," Miriam said.

"Not at all. Why do you say that?"

"I think you resent George's business success and want to take him down."

"Why would I resent him? I had a long, successful career in the law."

"He earned money. You're still poor."

"Is that what you think? That I'm envious of his money?"

"Yes, that's what I think. Now be quiet and let me work. With George about to be arraigned and Clyde dead..." her voice faltered, "...it's up to me to keep this place afloat."

"George may be away for a considerable time."

She bristled. "You think I don't know that? I'm not ignorant, Judge. George wouldn't rely on me to run the office if I were."

"I don't think you are ignorant, Miriam. Far from it. I think you are shrewd, too shrewd for your own good."

"What the hell's that supposed to mean?"

"You had it all figured out. You thought you could get away with it."

"Get away with what?"

"I think you know."

A plumber entered the office to complain about the crew he was working with. She dispatched him quickly. When he had left, Miriam scoffed. "Today's men are such pampered babies." She caught herself. "With the exception of George, of course. George is the finest man I've ever known."

"What about Clyde? What did you think of Clyde?"

She started to answer but stopped short and shook her head. "You almost had me there. I won't fall for your trap, Judge."

"What trap? All I asked was what you thought of Clyde. You worked closely with him for years."

She shook her head a second time. "No, I won't go there. Good try."

Jim spread his arms theatrically. "You're smarter than I am, Miriam. I surrender."

A little smile came to her face. "Bullshit, Judge. While I take an early lunch, you should work on your acting skills." She stood. "The office will be locked while I'm gone so you'll have to wait outside."

"Are you going to vanish, Miriam?"

"I wouldn't give you the pleasure."

Miriam was a woman who couldn't tolerate being off balance and he had upset her equilibrium, which pleased him. What would come next he couldn't predict.

He walked the intertwined streets of the light-industry district, oblivious to the beep, beep, of a delivery truck backing to a loading dock and the distant rumble of cars on I-93. In his ears: silence, total silence, except for a faint sound like tinnitus or the rustle of dry leaves.

Instinct had propelled him to Miriam's office, instinct told him to go back and wait for her. Now was the time to send her a message. The message: you can't get rid of me.

Miriam was at the office door fiddling with her keys when Jim appeared. She seemed surprised to see him. "Do you expect me to let you in?" she said.

"I do. You killed Clyde, didn't you?"

She found the right key and unlocked the door. She stepped in, letting Jim do so too.

"I suppose you're going to sit in one of those damn chairs until I answer your question, aren't you?"

"Yes."

"Why would I kill him? I loved him almost as much as I love George."

"Almost as much, but you love George more. You'd do anything to protect George, am I right?"

Miriam's face blurred with fury, affection, remorse, each emotion too fleeting to register.

Jim spoke softly, coaxing. "Miriam, I think I know why you killed Clyde but I want you to tell me. Why did you?"

Tears came to her eyes. She shook her head, too emotional to speak.

"Did he reject you? Did you make your love clear and he rejected you?"

"Of course not! I am not a lovesick teenager! I would never kill for such a silly reason!"

"Then why did you?"

"If I did, it was because Clyde was going to turn George in. He was about to destroy everything George had built!" Miriam grew agitated. "How could I let him get away with that?" She half-rose from her chair. "But I'm not saying I killed him."

Jim kept his voice soft and steady in response. "It sounds like you are, Miriam. If you did, it will go better for you if you get out in front of this."

"I want you to leave, Judge. Get out of my office and don't come back! You're no longer welcome here. It's up to me to keep this office afloat while George is gone, and you're getting in the way."

10

Pat came to Jim's for the night. They ate takeout from the local deli.

"Miriam came close to confessing today. I don't doubt she's guilty, but I need her confession to prove it."

"Pass the mustard, please, Jim."

"Any ideas?"

"My guess Miriam's waiting to see how George's arraignment goes. The arraignment's tomorrow, isn't it?"

"Yes, 10:30. He will confess to business crimes but not the murder. He swears he didn't kill Clyde. Ted said he was okay with that plea. We'll see."

The arraignment was held in the new courthouse in Woburn. Jim's courtroom had been in the old courthouse in East Cambridge. Jim still wasn't used to the change. Driving to the suburbs instead of taking the #69 bus to East Cambridge felt like driving out-of-state, and the new courthouse felt like a Holiday Inn.

George, standing with an ADA Jim didn't recognize, was sworn in by the judge, a woman Jim also didn't recognize.

The judge asked the court clerk to read the indictment, which consisted of seven counts, all of which centered on Holland Construction defrauding its customers.

"Mr. Holland, how do you plead?"

George answered without hesitation. "Guilty on all counts, Your Honor."

"Is bail requested?"

"No, Your Honor," the young ADA answered. "We don't believe that Mr. Holland is a flight risk. He voluntarily turned himself in to us, and he is supported by the distinguished former jurist, Judge Randall."

The arraignment judge nodded. "Very well. Mr. Holland, you have pled guilty to all seven counts in the indictment. I am setting a date a month from now for sentencing. Is there anything further we need to determine today? No? Then court is adjourned." A swift gavel and the judge disappeared out the back. When she had gone, George approached Jim.

"I'm glad that's over," George said.

"Pro forma."

"Not to me. Brand new. Got the adrenalin flowing."

"I've talked to the DA and we are close to an agreement on sentencing. You will get jail time but in view of your age and the circumstances of the case, we're nearing an agreement for two years, followed by house arrest, plus restitution. The customers who can be located will be paid the difference between what they thought they were getting and what they actually got." Jim looked at George for his reaction.

"I'm fine with that. Could be a lot worse."

"Where will you stay until sentencing?"

"With Sissy, making up for lost time. Will you be at the sentencing, Jim? I hope so."

"I'll be there."

"I am incredibly grateful to you."

"I'm not sure why. You are going to prison."

"Yes, but you could have turned your back on me, instead you helped me get through this. You stood by me. I'll never forget that."

Jim laid his hand on George's shoulder. "George, your heart hasn't changed. You gave in to the lure of money, 'hey, I'll cut a few corners here and there, and no one will be the wiser'. I don't think you ever expected this to go on for so long or get you mired so deeply in muck."

"See? No one else would bother to put what I did in context. I don't defend what I did, not for a nanosecond, but I don't think it sums up my whole life."

"Agreed. Now your role is just about over, but not Miriam's. She will be tried and I'm guessing, convicted."

"I'm very disappointed in her."

"She did it for you, George. She believed Clyde was about to blow the whistle and was determined to stop him."

"I still can't believe she did it for me," George sounded incredulous.

"And for Holland Construction which she helped build. But primarily for you. She was in love with you, George. Did you know that?"

"Never. It's hard for me to understand, but I believe you. What a damn shame. I'm not worth it. What about Pamela? What's going to happen to her?"

"I predict she will flee. Her only reason for coming back was to hurt you. I'm sure she didn't imagine getting tangled up in a murder. My guess is you'll never see her again."

"In a way, I feel sorry for her. She was starting to show signs of self-awareness, but my guess is she'll remain adrift for the rest of her life."

"I feel sorry for Miriam. She'll be in prison for most of the rest of her life for trying to protect you."

George shuddered. "Horrible thought: if she killed Clyde to stop him from blowing the whistle on me, ultimately I'm to blame for his death."

"You're to blame for risking the lives of your buildings' occupants but not for what Miriam did. That's on her."

At Jim's request, George left him alone in the courtroom. Sometimes when Jim had finished presiding over a trial, he would return to the empty courtroom and sit by himself, letting the trial replay in his mind. Now, alone in the courtroom after George's arraignment, his thoughts were of his childhood friend and he wanted to weep.

*

The din at Ipsa Loquitur was even louder than usual. Ted had to shout to be heard.

"Jim, are you listening?" Ted's voice cut through the din.

"No, sorry. What did you say?"

"How's your friend taking today?"

"I don't know. I haven't talked to him since the arraignment. How do you think it went?"

"By the book. No surprises."

"None for me either, except to see the youth of your ADA. I keep forgetting about the passage of time."

"You need another drink."

"I haven't finished my first one."

Ted signaled the bartender. "Better to be prepared than caught short."

"Is that an adage?"

"Absolutely. Those seven words contain all the advice you will ever need."

Jim feigned outrage. "Why didn't someone tell me that when I was young?"

"You wouldn't have listened."

"True. The young don't listen to the old. Did I tell you I'm seventy now?"

"Endlessly."

"Not true."

"You have talked of little else."

"Not so."

Refills arrived.

"How did we get started on this subject?" Jim asked.

Ted smiled. "Memory lapse, old timer?"

The din continued. The sounds of a courtroom ended as soon as a trial was over, the din at the Ipsa Loquitur was as endless as surf.

*

Miriam was charged with second degree murder for the killing of Clyde Martin. Jim thought that was a lenient charge – he would have opted for first degree if it were up to him. She went on trial five months later.

Jim was called as a prosecution witness. He told the truth about what he knew and what he didn't. When it came time for Jim to get personal, he expressed some sympathy for Miriam. "I think I understand why she did it. Her ultimate loyalty was to George Holland and she believed Clyde Martin was about to turn him in. She knows what she did was wrong even if she doesn't say so in court, but she did what she did for love and loyalty, which are in short supply these cynical days."

In the hallway after court adjourned for the day, Ted said to Jim, "You've become a softie in your old age, Jim."

"I've gained more sympathy for people. Life threats no one gently. We're all just doing the best we can. And that includes you, my friend."

"This is your lucky day. I'll treat you to lunch."

"Given that you're such a tightwad, I'm reluctant to pass up the chance, but I'm going home to sit in my most comfortable chair for as long as I can, moving as little as possible."

Aftermath

Miriam was found guilty and sentenced to twenty-five years to life with the possibility of parole in fifteen.

George was sentenced to two years in minimum security and six years of probation. Holland Construction went out of business after reimbursing as many defrauded customers as could be located.

Jim visited George in prison four times. Seeing George incarcerated made their childhood friendship seem like a mirage. Jim didn't want the memory to vanish entirely, so he didn't visit George in prison again. After George's release, whenever Jim suggested they get together, George made excuses. "I'm too ashamed, Jim. You knew me when I was a good person."

"You're still a good person. Don't give up on yourself."

"I'm sorry, Jim. Remember me as I was."

They haven't seen each other since.